SPINDLE

A FRACTURED FAIRY

TALE

By

J.E. Taylor

J.E. TAYLOR

SUPERNATURAL SUSPENSE
& DARK FANTASY AUTHOR

Spindle: A Fractured Fairy Tale © January
2023 J.E. Taylor

Will dragon's blood be enough to save the kingdom?

Long, long ago, a princess was born into the Kingdom of Light. She was said to be the most beautiful baby in all the world, and her tears turned into the morning dew. The king named her Aurora after the goddess of sunrise.

Royals came from far and wide to honor her birth, but one guest was not there to celebrate. When it was her turn to present a gift, the dragon queen offered something much darker. A curse that would claim Aurora on her twentieth birthday with the prick of a spinning wheel. Everyone in the kingdom, except King Henrick, would plummet into eternal darkness. Thus, the king would know the true meaning of loss.

Only three fae were left to bestow their gifts to the princess Aurora, and although they could not erase the dragon queen's curse, they could offer the kingdom a gift of hope.

Darkness would be banished with true love's kiss.

King Henrick hid Aurora with the fae in the middle of the kingdom's enchanted woodlands to keep her safe. But dragons are born of magic, too, and Aurora's hiding place was not far from the dragon's lair.

A Sleeping Beauty retelling with a little bite.

SPINDLE Chapter 1

AUTUMN FINALLY LET ME hunt without hunching over me like an overzealous mother bear. She had caught sight of a deer and went after it while I followed a bunny off our normal game trail. The scent of wet leaves itched my nose, but I tried to ignore it as I crept forward with my bow at the ready. The rabbit had to be around here somewhere. It had darted in this direction. I did my best not to make noise as I stepped through the brush, but I hadn't been blessed with the same light-footedness as the fae.

A twig snapped underfoot, sounding louder than normal with my attempt at near silence. And my furry prey hopped out of the brush. I aimed, tracking it while I blew out a stream of air. Then I let my arrow fly and held my breath. The arrow went straight through the rabbit's head. A clean death, if there ever was such a thing.

The sight of the rabbit's death twitch overshadowed my triumph of the hunt. I crossed to my quarry and kneeled, stroking its silky fur as the heat bled out of the body. A lump formed in my throat.

"I'm sorry, little one," I whispered.

"Why apologize?"

I startled, snapping my head toward the voice.

A boy.

I blinked at him as if he were an apparition.

His stance was confident, mature, and proud. He had to be older than me, perhaps even ten or eleven. His dark hair was pulled back in a severe ponytail that made his green eyes stand out. Flecks of gold glinted in his irises, captivating me with their beauty. His eyes seemed to shimmer, even with the canopy of trees shading us.

He tapped his ornate sword against the trunk of the tree as if his hands had different intentions than the rest of him. The tap-tap-tap pulled my gaze away from his face. His clothing was finer than a farm boy's, and the sword he held was ornate, as though it belonged to a knight.

I focused back on his face, completely forgetting what he had asked. "What?"

"Why are you apologizing to the rabbit?" He pointed his sword at the cooling carcass under my palm.

"Because he gave his life so we could survive." I gave him a look that should have told him what I thought of his question. I gripped the rabbit's ears and stood, holding it close to me in case he thought he was going to strip me of my kill. "Who are you?"

"Rory?" a voice called in the distance, and I jerked toward Autumn's call. When I glanced back, the boy was gone. My stomach tightened with disappointment, and I turned in a circle, trying to find evidence he had truly been standing in this little glen with me. My gaze dropped to the tree trunk. Very faint lines where he had been tapping were visible.

He must have been some kind of fae, or maybe even a ghost, because he vanished like a puff of smoke.

A red-haired, fair-skinned fae stepped through the trees into the small thicket. I smiled at her, but she

4

was clearly perturbed with me. She crossed her arms and arched a brow.

I held the rabbit up for her to see. "I got it."

Autumn sighed and allowed a smile. "That will make a nice rabbit stew." She crossed to me and slowed as she sniffed the air. Her gaze became guarded, and she slung her arm around my shoulders, steering me back toward her trodden hunting path.

I glanced over my shoulder one more time before that little area was out of sight. Scanning the woods, I still couldn't find that boy. Nothing moved.

"You shouldn't wander off like that, Rory," Autumn chastised me as we walked back home. "You know better. This is the trail you should stick to on our hunts." She pointed at the wooded path.

I nodded and glanced at the rabbit. Veering from our normal hunting grounds had been well worth the risk.

But even at seven, I knew to keep my opinion to myself.

Something deep down in the center of my soul told me I'd see that green-eyed ghost again.

YEAR AFTER YEAR, I sneaked away from the hunting path in search of that boy. He haunted my dreams, in a good way, but with each nighttime fantasy playing on the back of my eyelids, the longing to find him grew, and the doubt that he had only been a figment of my imagination created an unnamed fear in my heart.

Maybe today would be the day he reappeared. I stretched and stepped out the door to get away from the escalating argument inside. The fae were fighting over my lesson plans. Again.

Marabel, the eldest of the three fae sisters, wanted me to read today. Her hands seemed to speak a language of their own as she stressed the importance of storytelling. In the thick of the argument, her glasses had gone cockeyed on her face and strands of hair had fallen out of her gray bouffant as it bobbed with her animation.

Felicity, the dark fae with violet eyes and dark hair that nearly matched her skin, wanted me to cook. She was more regal in her mannerisms than Marabel, but her graceful animation was more fluid as she made her argument.

Then there was Autumn, the red-haired, cream-skinned fae. My favorite by far because she was the one who let me run around in the woods, hunting or making friends with the wildlife instead of keeping me locked up in the cottage like both Marabel and Felicity seemed to demand.

I silently slid my bow and quiver out of the corner. I was going exploring before any of them were the wiser. It had been almost eight years since I saw the green-eyed ghost in the woods, and I hoped this might be the day I'd find that elusive boy.

With the fae preoccupied, I stepped into the midst of the lush, enchanted forest. It was always bright and cheery here. Even the flowers seemed to sway when there wasn't a stitch of a breeze. The illusion of perfection surrounded us and even as I glanced over my shoulder at the three fae bickering about what my lessons were supposed to be, I knew I was blessed.

I took off in the direction I remembered meeting him. I caught sight of another rabbit and notched my arrow, slinking after it as I had been taught. It never even twitched his ears. I blew out a breath and let the arrow fly. I shot true, and the arrow pierced the rabbit's head, just as cleanly as all my kills.

I kneeled next to the rabbit and went through my ritual of feeling the last of the warmth bleed out of its body while I thanked it for its sacrifice. Although I loved the taste of freshly cooked meat, if I had my way, I wouldn't kill until I absolutely had to. This game killing thing was hard on a girl's soul. If I could, I would eat berries for the rest of my life, just to spare the animals. I stood with the rabbit in hand and gasped.

Narrowed green eyes stared at me down the edge of a sword aimed at my neck. He sniffed the air, and then the metal dropped to his side. His hair was shorter now than it had been eight years ago, but those golden-flecked green eyes that I had dreamed of every single night since I was seven were the same. A goofy smile appeared on his face, etching dimples into his cheeks and making his eyes sparkle.

"I did not think I would ever see you again, Rory," he said.

His voice had become deep, and hearing him say my name was like a cool piece of silk flowing over me. My knees buckled in a swoon, but I locked them and shook away the spineless sensation. His teeth flashed white from behind his soft, oh-so-kissable lips. He was even more handsome than I remembered.

He raised an eyebrow, as if he knew my private thoughts.

Heat filled my cheeks, and I cleared my throat. "I am at a disadvantage. You know my name, but I do not know yours."

"Z—" His eyes widened, and his gaze jerked beyond my shoulder. "I have to go. But I will see you again, Rory." He turned, bolting away as if a wolf were chasing him.

One would have thought there would be some sign that he had been real, but even the leaves in the direction he ran hadn't so much as shivered from the breeze he would have created.

"There you are!" Autumn broke through the thicket behind me.

I already knew the lecture that was coming, so I turned with the rabbit in my hand, giving her my best innocent grin.

"I may have to hide your bow and arrows," she grumbled and gripped the back of my neck to steer me back toward our little abode.

I did not understand her fear of these woods. What could be out here that would cause my favorite warrior fae to tremble? In fifteen years of hunting, I still had yet to run into anything as dangerous as the fae professed.

Beasts or no beasts, I would wander off the hunting path again. I just didn't know how long it would be until I could find my way back to my green-eyed ghost.

SPINDLE Chapter 2

"THE BIRTH OF A queen was supposed to be an exciting event. It started off that way, but soon fell into chaos when the Dragon queen showed up and placed a curse on the child. A curse that would plummet our kingdom into eternal darkness." Marabel recounted the story of the dragon queen's curse for the hundredth time. Her hands moved in broadly animated fashion and her gray hair bounced with each nod of her head.

I kept the smile plastered on my face and nodded from time to time, but my mind wasn't on this old fairy tale that she kept telling me. My mind was preoccupied with what I had overheard the fae chattering about earlier that morning. Something about a celebration for the princess, and maybe, just maybe, I would see my green-eyed ghost at the party.

I had never been outside the enchanted woods and was itching to go to the castle. To dress up in something stunning and dance the night away with a real man, ideally my famous woodland stranger. The forest animals didn't make good dance partners, despite their attempts at making me smile at their antics.

Felicity kneaded dough on the table and rolled her violet eyes at me before swiping a strand of her dark hair away from her face. I pressed my lips together at both the eye-roll and the track of flour that remained across her dark skin. She was just as tired as I was with this story.

"Are you listening?" Marabel stopped and stared at the two of us.

"Yes, ma'am," I answered. "You just said the curse on the princess would plunge the entire kingdom into darkness if she were to prick her finger on a spinning wheel."

"Yes, yes." She launched into a tirade about how the darkness would spread to every nook and cranny of the kingdom.

I glanced out the window, wishing for some reprieve so I could go out in the woods, where I was most comfortable. As if she heard my silent wish, Autumn strolled into the house with a freshly plucked duck for cooking held in front of her. Her crooked smile of triumph didn't deter Marabel from continuing to jabber.

Autumn flipped her auburn hair away from her face and leveled a cocked eyebrow at Marabel. "Give it a rest, sister."

Marabel's mouth dropped open at her sister's brazen comment.

Autumn handed Felicity the duck. "You're the only one who can make this taste like a feast," she added and wiped her hands on a cloth as she winked at me.

"No truer words have been spoken," Marabel said. "If I attempted to prepare it, we would get a much tastier meal by chewing on our leather shoes." She wiped her hands on her apron and started tidying up the place as if her sister hadn't just told her to be quiet.

I stifled a laugh and glanced at the fae folk. They were quite the trio, and life with them had been endless fun. Each one had taught me all their secrets, enough so that I could hunt for myself and prepare a feast, while spinning an entertaining tale. I knew how to mend socks and sew and even how to tend to our garden. I was ready to take on the world.

Unfortunately, none of them were ready for me to spread my wings, even after all these years.

The more I wandered, the more agitated they seemed to get. I was turning twenty in a couple of days and I had never seen the palace. Never mind exploring beyond our small cove carved in the woods; even on the hunting trips with Autumn, we stayed within the enchanted forest. I really wanted to experience what was out there. I wanted to explore our entire kingdom and not just this small crop of land.

As usual, they argued over how to prepare the duck. Even though Felicity was the only proper cook, they all had to put in their ideas before the three of them could settle on a direction. I took the opportunity to quietly slip away. I grabbed my favorite bow and the quiver of arrows leaning next to the door. It was my turn to commune with nature and possibly bring in a bounty that would last us a few more days than the meal Autumn had brought home.

I smiled as their continued bickering wafted out the window, filling the small clearing with their voices. As soon as I stepped into the woods, birds singing, chipmunks chattering, and owls hoo-hooing replaced the fae's squabbling. The familiarity calmed me as well as tickled my wanderlust, and I knew the exact direction I wanted to go.

I paused and glanced over my shoulder, half expecting Autumn to step out from behind a tree and reprimand me for wandering from the worn hunting trail. When she didn't, I headed in the direction that she always prevented me from going. She had never given me an actual reason we couldn't go beyond the magical boundaries. It always set my exploration itch into overdrive. My entire body tingled with the need to break the barriers the faeries had laid for me.

With none of the fae in sight, I picked up my pace, trying to be as light on my feet as possible, but I couldn't move silently the way Autumn did. Before I knew it, the forest thickened. I was farther beyond our normal hunting grounds, even farther than I had been when I met my green-eyed ghost. I even thought I felt a tingle of magic dance over my skin as I passed through an opening in a prickly thicket.

The ground became spongey under my feet, leaving a slick slime on the soles of my shoes. I slowed and studied my new surroundings as I tried to find more solid ground. The deep forest-green of the woods had transitioned to bright sunny flowers and brighter greens of swamp grass braided through the blossoms. It was almost as if the color popped much more here than it ever did in the enchanted forest. Not that the fae folk didn't have colorful surroundings, but this seemed much richer in contrast.

The squishy ground seemed to drive me toward a solid line of bushes in my quest for a dry surface to walk on. But I couldn't seem to break through the thick barrier. Just when I was about to give up, I spied a gap in the branches. I wiggled through and over the berm and nearly tumbled into a steaming body of water.

I straightened and scanned the oversized flowers of yellow, red, and blue that lined the pond. Their colorful reflections danced on the surface. Fluttering wings pulled my gaze to the tree limbs reaching out over the water, and my eyes widened at the size of the birds perched on the ancient wood. They were twice the size of the duck Autumn had brought home earlier.

My heart jumped in my chest at the chance to shoot a prize that big. It would feed us for a week. I reached for an arrow, pulling it from my quiver with slow precision, and notched it in my bow. I climbed up on the rocks at the edge of a sheer drop to the water that was at least three times my height.

I took a deep breath and tore my gaze away from the drop, focusing on the birds again. I took aim and shifted to steady my hand.

My darn slippers still had swamp muck on them, and I lost my balance.

A yelp ripped out of my mouth as I fell. I dropped the bow and grabbed for the rock, catching a small outcrop. The liquid sizzled when my bow and arrow hit the surface of the swamp. I stared in stunned silence as the wood burst into flames.

What I thought had been water was actually an acid pool. My heart thundered as my grip slipped from the small outcrop. I slid down the facing until I caught another small outcrop. I cried out, and I kicked the wall to find enough purchase on the rocks to get back to safety, but my shoes were too slippery.

I was too close to the surface and my fingers ached. The quiver on my back slipped off and when it hit the surface, a splash of acid doused my ankle. I screamed as pain nearly paralyzed me.

"Help!" I cried. Tears blurred my vision. I couldn't hold on much longer. As if fate was laughing at me, the grip I held tight to crumbled and I slid further toward certain doom. I scrambled for purchase and luck was with me this time. I caught a crevice and, although it bit into my skin, I screamed my triumph until acid engulfed my foot, and then my scream turned into a wail of agony.

Panic turned my breathing into harsh panting as I tried desperately to climb back up the rock high enough not to feel the burn again. If I perished in this acid bath, no one would know what happened to me. Marabel, Felicity, and Autumn would search forever and never find my body.

"Please help me," I whispered through a fresh set of tears as my fingers, now slick with blood, slipped on the small fissure. My life flashed before my eyes. All the hunting trips with Autumn. All the delectable treats I baked with Felicity, and all the stories Marabel and I created. Memories of my green-eyed ghost swarmed along with every dream of our future. All gone in a pouf of pain and fire.

The moment I lost my grip, something grabbed me around the

waist and lifted me from my pending death. My foot still throbbed, and from what I could see, it was a bloody, charred mess. But the pain faded with the sudden thrill of flying over the forest. I had a moment to wonder whether I died and then the flap of wings stirred the air around me, making my foot feel as if I had dipped it straight into the fires of hell.

Strong leathery talons held me, and when I glanced to the side, the edges of bright red, orange, and yellow wings filled my vision. The wings reminded me of bonfire flames. Stunning and dangerous all wrapped into a single image and my breath labored in my chest.

We descended into a field of white flowers and moss, and before I knew it, I was face down on the soft ground. The sweet scent of lilies swept over me, and I rolled, looking up at what had saved me.

My eyes widened, and I tried to scramble away, but my foot was too damaged from the swamp. I gasped and fell on my back, grabbing my leg as tears marred my vision. The dragon dipped his magnificent fire-orange head and sniffed me. His sharp green eyes shimmered with golden flecks, giving me such a strong sense of déjà vu. His snout traveled over my bloodied hands and my injured foot.

I couldn't tell whether he was going to finish what the swamp started or not.

When his gaze moved to mine, I think I stopped breathing. He lifted his head and then brought his talon-like claw to his mouth. His sharp teeth ripped his own flesh. I didn't have time to register shock before a drop of his blood the size of one of Felicity's pies splashed down over my injured foot and a second bathed my hands.

I cried out as paralyzing pain gripped my foot. It was far worse than the acid burn had been. My breath caught in my throat and then I started panting because I couldn't draw in enough air. All the while, the dragon watched, as if amused by my pain. I wanted to shoot an arrow right through one of his golden-flecked eyes.

Rolling onto my belly, I curled up with my forehead to the soft ground so the dragon could not witness the tears that bathed my face with warmth. I clasped my hands to my chest and silently prayed the beast would give me a quick death.

The agony faded into a tingle and I glanced at my hands. My fingers were no longer shredded from the rocks. There wasn't even a trace of my blood. I pushed back on my knees in case the tears in my eyes were showing me a trick. I turned them palms up and then palms down to make sure. But even with the sunlight shining down, my hands were pristine.

I uncurled my legs from beneath me, expecting the pain of my ruined foot to flare, but nothing happened. Sunlight warmed the unmarred skin of both feet. What had been a bloody, burned mess when we landed was now fully healed. I reached down and ran my fingers over the skin to validate what my eyes were seeing. The flutter of my fingers tickled, and I let out a surprised laugh.

A huff behind me stiffened my back, and I slowly turned toward the dragon. He still stared down at me, but this time he actually looked as if he smiled.

My gaze jumped to the talon he tore to bathe my wounds in his blood. His bloodstained talon. The gash he created had mended as surely as my hands and foot had.

Awe filled me, and I met his gaze. "Did you just..." I waved at my foot.

He dipped his snout and sniffed me again, but this time he seemed to rub the side of his nose against my cheek. I reached up and cupped his chin, pushing him away with a laugh. This encounter was nothing like the nightmarish stories Marabel had described.

I climbed to my feet and made my way around him, studying his stunningly vibrant colors. The entire time, his magical green eyes followed me.

When I settled back in the spot in front of him, I smiled. "Thank you."

Glancing at my surroundings, I had no idea how far off the path I was. I didn't even know which way home was, and my heart sank. I bit my lip and looked up at the dragon.

"You wouldn't happen to know the way to the fae village?" If I could get to the village, I could find my way back to our cottage.

He pointed his chin behind me, and I turned in the opposite direction of where we had flown from. I glanced back at his unique green eyes. A part of me wanted to stay with this beast, but I knew I had to get home before the three fae sent out a search party.

"Thank you again." I backed away.

Sadness filled his eyes as I moved away from him. I finally turned toward my destination once I had crossed most of the flower field, but turning away from the dragon had yanked at my chest.

I sighed and kept going, ignoring the pull of the beast.

SPINDLE Chapter 3

BEFORE I STEPPED INTO the woods at the far side of the flower field, a shadow hid the sun, and I glanced up at the underside of the dragon. His magnificent wings took him high enough to block out the light and then he veered in the opposite direction, away from where I was headed. A ride would have been more convenient, but I could just see the fairies' faces if we were to land in the small courtyard outside our cottage.

Marabel would fall in a dead faint. Autumn would grab her quiver of arrows and Felicity would start a fire in the oven to cook the dragon. I chuckled at the thought. I no longer had slippers, and I wasn't sure if I lost them to the swamp or to the dragon flight, but one thing was for sure, the forest floor was much less forgiving than the field had been.

The woods were thick, and by the time I reached the next poppy field, I was ready for the soft ground. This field was blue and gold as opposed to white, like the one the dragon left me in. It was stunning and the sweet floral scent blanketed the air, giving me a sense of relaxation and peace that I did not realize existed outside of our little cottage.

The ground felt fabulous on my feet after the forest floor and I took my time crossing, eyeing another set of woods with trepidation. By the time I reached the cottage, my feet were bound to be torn up enough that even slippers would hurt. So much for being comfortable at the party at the palace.

The next set of woods ended in a thick wall of thorn bushes that reached at least ten feet into the air above me. I followed along the bushes, but could not see a way through. When I doubled back, the same barrier held true. Sighing, I bent over and ripped some fabric from the hem of my tunic and wrapped each hand. I did the same to my feet and then stared up at the thorns.

With trepidation building in my chest like a lead weight, I reached up to grab a branch. The moment my fingertips touched the wood, the bush came alive. I yelped and tried to escape, becoming entangled, but it was futile. Before I knew it, vines wrapped around my arms and legs, pulling me into the sharp shards. Prickers pierced my skin in over a dozen places. The more I struggled, the more I bled.

"Let her go!" a deep, barking voice came from behind me.

The vines receded. I stumbled back, right into the powerful arms of the stranger who commanded the thorn bushes. He steadied me and I turned to face my savior.

Green eyes with golden flecks. I blinked at those familiar eyes. It wasn't just a mirror of the dragon's eyes, either. They were the eyes of my green-eyed ghost.

As he studied me, a crop of dark hair fell onto his forehead. He was built like the farm boys I saw tilling the fields on the outskirts of the fae borders, but his nails were as pristine as mine after a good scrubbing. He flashed a smile at me, and my knees nearly gave out. Something regal about him screamed royalty, and I fought the urge to bow.

My gaze fell on the equally familiar sword at his side. "Zee?" I finally squeaked out.

A dimple appeared in his cheek. "It's actually Zachary. I never got to finish telling you my name before your fae friend happened along." He glanced at the thorn vines. "These vines have a mind of their own." He nodded toward the thorny thistles and then glanced down at my exposed arms. "And it seems they have shown you no mercy." He reached for my hand. His touch was soft and tender as he inspected my wounds.

I was too thunderstruck by him to utter a word. My brain was still stuck on the fact his eyes were the same as the dragon's. But each stroke of his finger seemed to dull the pain of my cuts. It was as if he were magically wiping them from my skin. It took me a moment to get my senses back, and I pulled my hand from his grip.

I had the feeling that if he hadn't come around, the vines would have strangled me to death. "Thank you for stopping them."

He licked his lips and shrugged as if it were no big deal. "What are you doing roaming around in the Dragon Realm?" He raised an eyebrow.

I gasped and stepped back, right into the sharp prickers, wincing as I arched away from the shards. "D-Dragon Realm?"

"Yes." He cocked his head. His eyes sparkled with the same interest I remembered him looking at me with before. "Did you know you smell like sunshine and morning dew?"

I wasn't sure how to respond to his sweetness, even with the alarms going off in my head at the fact I was in the Dragon Realm. In every story Marabel had told me of dragons, they were vicious murderers that killed for sport. But considering I had been saved by one, I couldn't reconcile the stories with the real thing. Especially with the golden flecks in his eyes sparkling in the sunshine, just like the dragon's eyes.

"Were you the one who saved me from the acid swamp?" I asked, instead of acknowledging his strange compliment.

His cheeks turned rosy, and he glanced away with a nod.

Holy cow. My green-eyed ghost was a *dragon.* That explained so much. "And you were keeping an eye on me as I crossed through the poppy fields?" I asked, remembering the shadows he created when flying overhead.

He shuffled his feet. "Yes."

"Why?" I blurted. "Why didn't you shift before and tell me who you were? You scared the hell out of me." I swatted his arm.

"My fierce little huntress scared?" he teased with a grin that was swoon-worthy. "Besides, I could always tell when you were close. Your scent is intriguing and very, very unique. I just never imagined you would be on *this* side of the wall." He looked up at the prickers and then down at me. "So, beautiful one, why did you come to *my* kingdom?"

Heat rushed to my cheeks. It was my turn to shuffle my feet. If I could have scrambled over the wall of prickers, I would have just to get away from this overwhelming pull in the center of my stomach. The sudden image of being caught in his arms with his lips on mine was too tempting. I stared at the ground as the rest of his words sunk in. "Your kingdom?"

"I am Prince Zachary of the Dragon Realm." He waved at the surroundings. "So yes, my kingdom. Why, dear Rory, did you breach the wall?"

"I was just following a hunting trail," I said softly, lost in his piercing gaze. "I did not know I crossed into the Dragon Realm."

He hooked his finger under my chin and tilted my head so I would meet his gaze. He stepped closer as if he had the same rampant thoughts I was. His thumb brushed my bottom lip.

"You are forbidden." He breathed the words as he dipped his head down toward mine.

Forbidden? His whispered words smacked sense into me, and I placed my hands on his chest and leaned back to avoid the kiss he was about to deliver. As much as my inner voice screamed at me for putting this moment on pause, everything I had been taught rushed back, and along with it came my sense of self-preservation.

"I need to get home." I sucked my lower lip between my teeth.

His eyes widened with surprise at my rebuff. From the looks of him, no one ever refused the prince. He blinked and then inhaled and stepped back with a nod. "Now that you know who and what I am, will I ever see you again?"

The longing in his eyes sent my heart beating more frantically than it already was. I opened my mouth to say I hoped so, but nothing came out. I wasn't sure what would happen if he got caught crossing into the fae lands. Dragons were not welcomed, and I didn't want to start another war, especially considering it had been the dragon queen who cursed the princess, if Marabel's stories held any truth.

The prince took another step back and his features hardened. "Do you not wish to see me again?"

I sighed. "You are the green-eyed ghost that haunts my dreams. I *always* want to see you," I said, and the hard lines of his jaw softened with a grin. "But if you ever get caught in the fae lands, I'm not sure what would happen to you."

His gaze traveled up the thorn bushes. "I have rarely been beyond this wall. It is just as forbidden as letting you leave." His eyes found mine. "But you would not survive a night here, either." He reached his hand out beyond my head and winced as he laid his palm on the sharp prickers. "Let her pass," he said.

The bushes parted, leaving an opening a little wider than my shoulders. I hesitated at the sight of blood dripping down his wrist. Instead of darting through the hedges, I took his cheeks between my palms and pressed a kiss to his lips.

His free arm wound around my waist, and he pulled me against his well-chiseled body. Our lips parted and our tongues mingled in a slow dance that left me breathless. If I didn't stop right now, I would never leave this bliss.

I pulled away and darted through the bushes before I changed my mind.

"I will see you again, Rory," he said with conviction, and then removed his hand from the bush.

It closed like the slamming of a door, and my heart squeezed. I took a step closer to the thorny wall, and the vines reached toward me in that malignant way that spelled death.

SPINDLE-A FRACTURED FAIRY TALE

SPINDLE Chapter 4

EACH STEP AWAY FROM the thistle bushes crashed through me as if a boulder were being slammed into my stomach. I kicked at the dirt, wincing at the stub of my bare toe.

I trudged through the green field until I found a road and then headed away from the direction of the Dragon Realm. But all I could think about was

Zachary and the way his kiss had made my entire body tingle with desire.

I only knew the horror stories that Marabel, Autumn, and Felicity had recounted. The dragons had once ruled half of the kingdom, but after the dragon king died, war broke out. Villages on both sides were destroyed, and the barrier Zachary let her through had been erected. But the stories said a wall built by fae magic had been erected so the dragons could not leave their lands.

But if the fae had built that wall of thorns and vines, why had a dragon commanded it? Why had dragon blood opened the wall?

My steps faltered. I stopped in the middle of the road, mulling over all I had been fed over the last twenty years.

"There you are!" Felicity's sharp voice carried on the wind.

I looked up to see the three fae rushing down the road toward me, their faces masks of relief. As they neared, that relief changed into concern.

"What in the king's name happened to you?" Marabel asked as she flitted around me.

I glanced down at myself. My arms still had bloody welts. My feet were bare and nearly blackened with dirt. My tunic was ripped, and the swaths tied around my hands were stained with blood from the thorn punctures.

"I was hunting," I said, still staring at my hands.

Autumn pulled something from my hair and waved it at me. "Where did you go?" Her voice thundered in my face.

I licked my lips and scanned each curiously angry face, peering at me. "I... uh." I shuffled my feet, unsure why I wasn't being honest with them. I glanced down at the ground.

Autumn stepped close and sniffed my hair. She nearly stumbled backward. Her mouth popped open, almost as wide as her eyes. "You smell like dragon blood."

I let out a high-pitched laugh. "Funny story," I started, trying to wipe the horror off her face. "Dragons aren't as awful as you three have painted them to be."

It was as if the world had stopped spinning. All three fae stood rigidly, staring at me with eyes like saucers and chins dangling.

"One saved me from an acid swamp," I blurted.

Three sets of eyebrows arched.

"And he healed my wounds and let me go," I added, trying to erase the panic flitting in their eyes. "And then he saved me from the thorn wall. And let me pass through." I rubbed my hands together, peeling off the fabric wraps, so I didn't have to look at the shock on their faces any longer.

"You went through to the Dragon Realm?" Marabel squeaked.

"That is what I am trying to tell you. I have no idea how I got over there. I didn't cross through the thorn bushes to get there." I chewed on the inside of my mouth, trying to remember how I had gotten in if the thistle barrier truly surrounded the land, but all I remembered was following a wildlife trail.

Autumn and Felicity each grabbed an upper arm, and they marched me back to the cottage without a word. Smoke drifted out the windows of our little abode. Felicity squealed, dropped my arm, and flew inside. We all followed.

The duck she had started to cook when I left was now a charred shell. Thankfully, it had not fallen off the spit and started the rest of the cottage on fire, although the amount of smoke still wafting out the windows and doors would seem to indicate that it had come close to demolishing our home.

A dress in the center of the room was covered in soot and a cake on the counter that had partly fallen remained. The horror at the mention of a dragon did not compare to the devastation painted on each of their faces at the condition of their little world.

Marabel burst into tears, covering her face. Autumn fell into the nearest chair as if she had been shot by an arrow, and Felicity stood still in the center of the room, just staring at the overcooked bird.

"Today was supposed to be perfect," Autumn whispered.

A chill skittered down my back. This was my doing, but the guilt making my stomach roll didn't quite wipe out the questions accosting my mind. "Did the fae make that barrier?" I asked, because I could not get that to settle right in my head.

All three fae turned toward me, exchanged glances, and nodded in unison. They looked as if they had secretly eaten the last piece of holiday pie.

I crossed my arms and cocked a skeptical eyebrow.

"Well... technically, the dragons created the wall of thorns, but the fae hold it in place. Otherwise, it would have grown rampant through our kingdom and swallowed every living creature outside of the dragons," Marabel said.

I narrowed my eyes at her. There were so many holes in her version of the truth that it would look like Swiss cheese if I let them continue. "I need to clean up." I headed toward the bath at the back of the house to clean the grime off from my walking and bleeding in the Dragon Realm.

I hand-pumped a bucket of water and poured it into the warmer before getting another bucket. When I returned with the second bucket, the first was just warm enough to not chill me to the bone. I let the warmer drain into the tub before plugging it and pouring the second bucket. Rinse. Repeat. By the time the tub was nearly filled, I was ready for the bath.

It took a fair amount of scrubbing to get the grime off my body and out of my hair. By the time I was done, the water had turned a disgusting cloudy brown from the dirt. I unplugged the tub, waiting until the soiled water drained completely before closing the drain and adding the last bucket from the warmer to finish my soak.

The last batch nearly scalded, but I forced myself to soak in it, and ease any knotted muscles in my legs and back. My mind wandered to the kiss I had shared with Zachary. When the water was nearly cool, I scooped up handfuls and ran it over my shoulders and hair, wiping off any remaining dirt. By the time I stepped out of the tub, I felt cleaner than I had in weeks.

I towel-dried my hair and wrapped a robe around me. The clothing I had been wearing was too soiled to wear again. I scrubbed them clean in the remaining water before I hung them on the line to dry.

When I stepped back into the heart of the house, it was as if dinner had never burned. A magnificent dress hung in place of the one covered in soot. A tall cake sat on the counter, and a duck roast sat on the table, with all the fixings.

It seemed my fairy godmothers had decided that magic was needed to save the day, which was just as rare as me wandering away from the cottage. I reached for the dress.

"Not yet, child. That is for the palace tomorrow night."

I had almost forgotten about the ball. "Do you think the dragon I met will be there?" I asked as I took a seat at the table. As soon as the question fell from my lips, I knew the answer.

"Dragons are not welcome in King Henrick's court," Felicity said with such a cool voice that I glanced up from the feast before me. "I doubt one would be so bold after the last time." She dug into the meal with no more explanation.

When the meal was over, the cake was set on the table before me. Golden letters glistened in the sweet frosting, wishing me a happy birthday. "You are a day early." I glanced at them.

"We will be at the castle tomorrow night for the celebration." Felicity nodded toward the cake. "Go on. Make a wish!"

Twenty candles burned on the top tier and I stood, closed my eyes, and made a wish to see Zachary again, to dance with him until the sun rose. I took a deep breath and blew. Every candle went out.

I grinned. If only it were that easy.

Marabel, Autumn, and Felicity danced around me, still singing "Happy Birthday." They would continue until I devoured a piece of their sweet confection. I cut a small slice and put it in my mouth.

Their singing stopped as they waited for my judgment of their masterpiece.

The cake literally melted into a sweet, tangy mixture of strawberry and vanilla in my mouth. I leaned back, closed my eyes, and took a moment to savor the goodness. I smiled and opened my eyes to their rapt attention.

"You've outdone yourselves with this one."

Felicity grinned as if I had given her a golden four-leaf clover, and both Marabel and Autumn clapped happily. We all tore into the delectable cake as though we didn't have a care in the world.

Thunder clapped outside the window, making all of us jump. It felt like a foreshadowing of doom. If the world was going to end tomorrow with the princess's curse, I was hell-bent on seeing Zachary one last time before the gauntlet dropped on humanity.

SPINDLE Chapter 5

I TOSSED AND TURNED all night, too excited to sleep, so I climbed out of bed before daybreak and slipped out of the cottage. The skies were just lighting up like a rainbow. The clouds that had crowded the sky the previous evening had spilled their wares and left, as if they knew that today of all days needed to let the light shine. A strange sensation tingled in the air, as if it knew the time in the light was ending.

I shivered and rubbed my arms as I made my way back toward the pricker bushes holding the dragons in their territory. The sun broke over the horizon, nearly blinding me. I squinted as I followed the path the sun lit.

In the distance, a form emerged from the rays of light, and I blinked to make sure it wasn't just the blinding dots from the sun playing tricks on my mind. As I got closer, the form of a man came into focus. But with the light framing him, his face hid in shadows.

Caution flags flared in my mind. This couldn't be the prince. Not on this side of the barrier. It was too dangerous for him to be on this side. My heart clanged in my chest at the thought. Encountering strangers on a deserted path was just as harrowing, and I glanced around for any escape route. The trees were closer to the approaching man than they were to me. But if I could get there, the woods would give me cover.

I sprinted toward the trees. Halfway across the field, I caught movement near me to my right. I took my eyes off the wood line at the same moment a body slammed into me, taking me to the ground in a roll. I struck out blindly until hands grabbed my wrists and slammed them on the ground by my head.

"What. The. Hell," a breathless voice above me said.

I tossed my hair out of my eyes and Zachary's bright-green eyes looked down at me with exasperated humor. My mouth popped open as I stilled. My chest heaved with the exertion, and Zachary's grip on my wrists loosened.

"What are you doing here?" I asked when I finally caught my breath.

He grinned. "I told you I would see you again."

With his body still draped over me, I was helpless to fight off the charm in that smile. It made my heart go into the same pitter-patter that the run had, but this time, instead of an adrenaline rush, heat enveloped me.

His gaze dropped to my lips and then he rolled off me, taking a seat in the grass next to me. I didn't move. I just stared at the deep-blue sky above me, waiting for my skin to cool before I sat up. When I did, I hand combed the leaves out of my hair and glanced at him, leaning back on a single elbow with a blade of the long grass between his teeth. Prince Zachary lounging on the grass like a commoner sent my temperature to high.

He studied our surroundings with interest, but it was nothing compared to the way his eyes shined when they landed on me. It was as if he had swallowed the sun, and light naturally found the golden chips in his irises.

"You are taking a risk being here."

He laughed. A full throaty sound that I could get used to, and I was sure I would hear in my dreams for weeks to come.

"I have to say, despite the reaming I will get from my mother when I get home, tackling you in the grass was worth it."

"And yet you moved away from me." I cocked my head and gave him a sly smile.

"Is the lady inviting a kiss?" He rolled onto his hands and knees, crawling toward me like a predator.

I giggled and shuffled back, but he caught me by the ankles and crawled up my body in a way that sucked the breath from my lungs. His touch was light as he ran his fingers up my calves. And then he crawled the rest of the way and settled on top of me. His weight felt good, and we molded in all the right places.

"Why, dear lady, you seem to be a naughty vixen at heart," he purred, and his mouth found mine before I could launch a protest.

The kiss silenced any argument I could come up with in my head to stop where this was leading. The attraction between us was as raging as the fire of a dragon's breath. He took my cheeks gently in his palms and let out a gruff groan as the kiss deepened.

His hands flowed slowly down my neck and if he had stopped there, I would have been content to kiss him until the moon rose. But his exploration did not stop. He ignited me with desire. His lips left mine to trail down my throat and into the vee of my shirt.

A rustling in the bushes pulled us both out of the moment. His nostrils flared as a rabbit hopped out from cover and twitched its nose at us before continuing across the field.

It was enough for me to come to my senses. When the prince leaned in to start again, I gently pressed my hand to his chest.

"I'm sorry. As much as I enjoy...this, I don't really know you."

He covered my hand with his and closed his eyes, taking a deep breath as he rolled onto his back next to me, accepting my not-so-valiant request to stop.

"I want to know you," he said softly, studying the leaves on the trees above us. "But I cannot have you risking your life by sneaking into my territory." He turned his head and met my gaze. He lifted my palm and placed a kiss in the center of my hand.

"And I cannot have you risking your life by sneaking into mine." I rolled on my side and propped myself up on my elbow to look down at him.

He glanced at me and cocked his eyebrow. "I could just ravage you right here, right now, you know."

I smiled. "I think you would already have done that if that was your intention."

"Mmmm. Are you so sure it isn't? I am a dragon, after all." He didn't move a muscle to make good on his thinly veiled threat. "And you are what I covet most."

"Oh. You covet me?" I put my hand to my forehead. "Whatever shall I do?"

He snorted laughter. "You do not strike me as the damsel in distress type, despite your misadventures yesterday."

I chuckled. I certainly was not a damsel in distress. I knew my way around a bow and a sword fairly well. "I am pretty good with a bow. Although my favorite one was eaten by your swamp."

"I shall make you another." He wrapped his arm around me, bringing me closer. "What else do you want?"

"I want my birthday wish," I said.

Sparks danced in his eyes. "And what wish would that be?" He traced a chilling path across my back with his fingers.

"I want to dance with you at the king's ball tonight," I said.

His lighthearted smile faded. "Oh Rory, I am so sorry to have to disappoint you."

"I know. Dragons, even attractive prince dragons, are not welcomed in King Henrick's kingdom." His stomach muscles twitched under my fingertips as I traced lazy circles over his loose shirt.

"I'm not so sure I could stay in human form if I went anyway," he said in a dark tone. "I might be inclined to eat King Henrick."

I blinked and pulled away from Zachary.

"King Henrick killed my father. Took his blood to heal his ailing wife." His tone carried the bitterness of growing up without a father as he stared up at the sky. "If he had just asked, I'm sure my father would have given him some of his blood, but the bastard got greedy. He wanted to slaughter another king for the betterment of his kingdom." He licked his lips and glanced at me. "My mother has never been the same."

I couldn't think of anything worse than losing the one you loved. It must have shown on my face, because Zachary propped himself up and pulled me into another kiss. This one tender and sweet and everything a girl could ever hope for in a kiss.

He pulled back and studied my eyes as though they held the secrets of the world. "I want to learn all your guarded secrets."

"I have no secrets," I said, and closed the distance.

His hand glided down my side, all the way to my knee, and he pulled me on top of him. His hands drew up around my waist as the kiss deepened. Beneath me, I could feel his hardness form between my straddled legs. He slowly ground against me, moving me in small circles. Those golden flecks in his eyes turned almost as hot as he was making me.

He tightened his jaw and closed his eyes. "You are forbidden," he said, almost as if it were a reminder to himself. "Innocent. Sweet. And oh, so damn edible."

His eyes flashed as he opened them, and I almost saw the dragon forming. I pulled back in alarm.

He chuckled, holding me tightly in place. His hips still circled slowly under me. Enough to bring forth a rush of wetness between my legs. I had never had thoughts of losing my innocence before I met Zachary. And now that was all I could think of.

Zachary stilled beneath me and closed his eyes, pressing his lips together. His eyes opened, and he stared at the sky. "Someday I will show you bliss, but that won't be today." He met my gaze. "My mother is calling and if I don't go..." His eyes filled with instant regret as he moved me off his lap. Zachary cupped my cheek and gave me a soft peck on the lips. "I will see you again, Rory," he vowed. And then he was up and was gone before I could straighten out my clothing and get to my feet.

Disappointment scratched over my heated skin, and I kicked myself for falling so easily into his arms. It was as if fate was forcing us to do things that put us in harm's way. After all, I had ventured out alone this morning with the sole goal of finding Zachary. He apparently had the same impulse.

Damn that sexy prince.

If I didn't watch myself, I'd certainly be eaten by a dragon.

SPINDLE Chapter 6

I TOOK MY TIME on my way back to the cottage. When I entered the glen, the fae were already dashing about, getting ready for tonight's festivities. When Marabel saw me, she grabbed me and ushered me inside with no comment as to my whereabouts. Thankfully, my routine included a morning walk and the timing of my return worked.

Before I spoke, they were already slipping me into the silky dress and tightening the corset until I could barely breathe. The sky-blue satin shimmered, and I smiled at the image in the mirror, even with my blonde hair windblown and knotted from my morning adventure. I could not envision being led around a dance floor by anyone other than Zachary.

A chair slid against the back of my knees, and I fell into the cushion as the three fae flitted around me.

"Should we braid her hair or curl it?" Felicity started brushing the tangles out with an efficiency that made me wince with each yank.

"Braid," said Autumn at the same time Marabel said, "Curls."

Marabel brought out a table with powders and colored chalk and sat right in front of me as if she were going to make me up like the court jester. I put my hand up and shook my head as she brought a powder puff straight toward my face.

"No thank you," I said to her, knowing it would probably hurt her feelings. But I never got the hang of make-up, and I did not want to look strange on my first foray into a royal ball.

"But..." she started.

"She is beautiful without all that fake stuff." Autumn sided with me for a change.

"I agree," Felicity added. "Even with her hair a mess, she would be the most stunning girl at the ball." She yanked at a few strands that framed my face and wrapped them around a tube that she left in place. She did the same with the other side and continued until I looked like a strange version of a porcupine.

She stepped back with a satisfied nod, stepped away for a moment, and when she returned, she had a plate of food that she handed to Marabel.

"Let Marabel feed you so you don't get anything on the dress, okay?"

"Um. Okay." I didn't have much choice in the matter and before I knew it, I was so full that I had to wave off the next pastry Marabel offered. Not a speck fell on the dress, either. If I had been left to eat on my own, I probably would have had at least one stain from a falling bite.

Felicity and Autumn raced about the cottage, dressing in their own clothing suited for court. Felicity returned to me and started pulling the tubes out of my hair. Little ringlets fell, framing my face and falling over my shoulders. She grinned at the effect and then went back to styling my hair.

She finally had Marabel bring a mirror out. She had done a stylish updo that included intricate braids interspersed with corkscrew curls, and the effect made me gasp with delight.

"You will outshine the entire royal court!" Felicity said as she studied me.

Heat filled my cheeks. I only wanted to impress one person, and he would not be there. I wished I could run to the glen where I found him this morning, just to show off this magnificent outfit. Although I was sure by the time I left him, I would be a hot mess.

I smiled at the thought. "Thank you." I glanced at the three fae.

Before they whisked me out of the cottage, I snuck a swipe of frosting from what was left of the cake on the counter. After all, it was my birthday cake and I wouldn't be able to have a piece until well into the evening.

At least, if the curse was a farce. Otherwise, I'd never see that sweet cake again.

I sucked the frosting from my finger as we stepped outside. I drew to a halt at the sight of an ornate golden carriage that reminded me of the flecks in Zachary's eyes. It was far too fancy to be from the modest fae realm we lived in. I had a moment where I thought Zachary would step out and hold the door for me. But that small daydream was ruined when Felicity swung the door open and waved me inside.

A measure of disappointment filled me, but at least my smile didn't falter. I climbed inside, followed by Autumn, Marabel, and Felicity. Their excitement created static in the air around them, sending little sparks of happiness flying around the inside of the carriage.

We lurched forward, and so did my heart. I was headed to the palace. Toward a night with a precarious ending. Tonight, the kingdom would celebrate the princess's twentieth birthday, and it would either end with too much wine, dance, and song, or it would end in ruin as the curse uttered so long ago blanketed the land.

The closer we got, the quieter the fae got. And the louder the ruckus outside the carriage. People shouted blessings as we passed, devotions for the curse to be lifted and the kingdom spared.

"Why do they shout prayers at us?" I asked the fae.

"They shout at all the carriages that are heading to the celebration in the hopes it will somehow lift the curse." Marabel's eyelids fluttered like they had when she told me that the fae had built the barrier between us and the dragons.

Marabel was not being totally honest, and neither Felicity nor Autumn dared to look at me.

"Am I missing something important?"

"No, no, sweetie." Marabel patted my leg and the three fae traded tense glances.

"What is it?" The exasperation in my question brought all three pairs of eyes to mine.

Marabel wrung her hands. "It's just... just that there hasn't been a big event like this since..." She glanced out the window. "Since the princess was cursed. And I'm sure we aren't the only ones who are a little on edge." She gave me a tight smile that I'm sure was supposed to calm me, but it just made this worse.

For the first time, I saw unease in them, and it wasn't from an ill-timed joke like sometimes happened at the cottage. This was true discomfort. I had no idea how nervous they were about this day until that very moment. "Everything will work out," I said, and it was my turn to pat her knee.

"Oh, child, I certainly hope so." She traded a glance with the other fae, who nodded in unison. This time, their smiles were much more natural.

The carriage came to a halt in front of a heavily guarded set of stairs. The door was yanked open by a stern-looking man in chainmail. His other hand stayed on the hilt of his sword. It was a little more than concerning, and I understood the fae's unease on the ride. It wasn't until his gaze landed on me that he seemed to soften. He stepped back with a grand bow.

Trumpets blew on the top of the stairs as Marabel, Autumn, and Felicity stepped out of the carriage. The guard offered his hand to help me out and then bowed again as if I were royalty. The steps were empty except for the men standing guard and the road behind us was absent of anymore carriages.

A chill climbed my spine as I navigated the stairs behind the fae. Guards rushed to open the doors, and we entered the massive castle throne room that was bigger than anything I had ever seen. The crowd milled on the floor and on a pedestal opposite the grand staircase sat King Henrick and Queen Lila.

Both sported severe expressions, as if they had not had a moment of peace in decades. The queen once may have been beautiful, but she looked like nothing more than a dried husk, with mousy-gray hair and lips as thin as lines. King Henrick looked no more impressive than his queen, with a belly that screamed of excess and a graying beard that looked as if someone had attempted to trim it but had failed. His hair was no better, sticking out in random tufts on an otherwise balding head.

The one endearing thing I noticed was that they held hands. It was such a small detail, but one I noticed right away.

The trumpets blared behind us, so loud I nearly tumbled down the stairs. I turned to see who was entering the grand ballroom, but just like in the street below, no one was behind us. When I turned back, all eyes were on the four of us, and both the king and queen were on their feet.

The dullness that had settled over them when I first laid eyes on them seemed to shatter and the king's bright smile lit up the room. The queen covered her mouth as if she were truly overwhelmed.

A hush fell over the crowd as the last of the trumpet blare faded and the sea of people parted, leaving a clear path between us and the king's pedestal. A chair next to the queen's was empty, and I glanced around, trying to guess which face in the crowd was the princess.

"Come." Felicity grabbed my hand. Autumn grabbed the other and Marabel moved behind me and fluffed my dress so it wouldn't catch on the stairs.

Everyone stared at me and I tried on a smile, but it felt so foreign. I did not like this attention. Especially with the king and queen rushing across the floor to meet us. The fae must really have done something sensational to get this type of attention.

When I neared the bottom of the stairs, I scanned the curiosity in every face of the crowd, and my gaze landed on a very familiar face. My heart tripped, and I stumbled right into the king's arms.

A collective gasp filled the air and the heat of embarrassment painted my cheeks. I was sure I was as red as some of the ballgowns. He steadied me back on my feet, and I shot Prince Zachary a quick look. He winked at me with a smirk. I forced my focus back on the king.

"I'm sorry, Your Majesty." I curtsied.

King Henrick smiled down at me in such a warm manner, it was as if he had wrapped a soothing blanket around me. "You are more beautiful than I ever imagined." He stepped back and looked me over from crown to toe and back.

I gawked at him like a damn fool, but that was abruptly interrupted by the queen as she threw her arms around me and pulled me into a tight hug. I glanced at the one responsible for me losing my balance. The smile on Prince Zachary's face faded as his gaze bounced between me, the king, and the queen. The seriousness carved into his features made me want to rush over to him and wrap my arms around him. I wanted that playful smile back, but Zachary seemed just as perplexed as me.

"My dear Aurora, it is so good to finally have you home," the queen whispered in my ear.

I imagined my face sported the same shock as Zachary's. I pulled away, nearly falling on the stairs behind me. "Ex...cuse me?" I stuttered and looked at Marabel, Autumn, and Felicity.

"Welcome home," King Henrick said with a broad grin.

This time, I sat down on the steps and just stared up at the king and queen, dumbfounded by their words. *Home?* My home was in the enchanted forest with Marabel, Autumn, and Felicity. Not in this oversized monument.

Autumn kneeled before me and took my hands. "Child, you *are* Princess Aurora, heir to the Kingdom of Light. King Henrick asked that you be protected from the dragon queen until your twentieth birthday."

"And you couldn't have given me a warning?" The fae's duplicity made my skin feel like a million ants were marching across it.

Autumn traded a glance with Marabel and Felicity and then met my gaze. "We could not. We took a potion that silenced us whenever we felt the need to divulge your true identity. We were not to speak of it until the king and queen welcomed you back into their home." She squeezed my hands, and the sincerity in her eyes quelled my uneasy itch.

I blinked, still numb from their words. *I* was the cursed princess? It took a moment to sink in, and then I looked around at the crowd watching this very spectacle.

I glanced back at the king and queen and cleared my throat. "I don't understand. You are my parents?" I climbed back to my feet, waving away any help from the fairies. I didn't know whether to be grateful or furious. They had, after all, abandoned me my whole life and put a gag order on my caretakers.

They nodded. "We needed to ensure your safety after these three powerful fae countered the dragon queen's curse. We did not know if she would make good on her threats and neither of us could bear the thought of you being hurt, so we felt you would be safer in their hands." King Henrick waved to Marabel, Autumn, and Felicity.

I considered his words and the sincerity in his deep-brown eyes. "And you and your armies could not protect me in this fortress?" I waved my hand at the palace surrounding us.

He glanced around. "We are not infallible. The day of your christening taught us that," he said. "And while it was a hardship on us, you were safe, which is all that truly matters." He turned around toward the rapt crowd. "Come, it is time for celebration." His voice boomed in the hall. The music started as we made our way toward the pedestal.

Zachary stepped out of the crowd as we passed. "Princess, may I have this dance?" He offered his hand before any of the guards surrounding us could intervene.

I stopped and took his hand. Just the idea of being in his arms was enough to send my heart racing.

"There are other suitors..." the queen started and pointed toward a group of men nearest the thrones.

"I would like to dance with *this* suitor." I smiled and allowed Zachary to lead me to the middle of the dance floor despite the frowns that formed on the king and queen's faces, as well as the confusion reflected on Marabel, Autumn, and Felicity's faces.

"Princess," Zachary said with almost a growl and bowed his head. Then he pulled me against his chest and planted his palm at the small of my back, keeping me in place. He moved with grace as he twirled me around the floor.

My heart thrummed in my chest, and I could not tear my gaze away from his very intense green eyes. This is what I had wished for, but there was a tension in Zachary that hadn't been there earlier. It bordered on hostility.

We moved around the floor in tight circles, weaving in and out of the other people trying to do the type of dancing I was accustomed to in the fae village. This was not the same. This was something both exciting and dangerous.

"You didn't know," he whispered almost accusingly, just above the music.

Whatever spell he had on me broke, and the story about his father flooded back into my head. *I was the daughter of the man who killed his father.* I slowly shook my head. "I didn't know. As far as I am concerned, the enchanted forest is my home, not this monstrous palace." I leaned back, studying the tight set of his lips. "Did you?"

The corner of his lip twerked upward, and his eyes softened. "No. I did not have the slightest clue. Had I, you would have been dead either by the acid pool or by my fire, and I would never know this ache in my chest or the fact you cloud my every thought."

I planted my foot and forced him to stop this maddening spin he'd swept me up in. He pulled me closer, staring down at me. Heat enveloped me as though I had stepped right into the heart of a dragon flame. His eyes shimmered, and he licked his lips as his gaze moved from mine down to my mouth and the memory of our kiss flushed my skin.

A guard's hand came into view and landed on his shoulder.

We both stiffened.

"It's time for the princess to take her rightful seat," the guard said. There was no leeway in his request, or the tight hold he had on Zachary's shoulder.

I gripped Zachary's hand tighter, not willing to let go just yet, especially after his declaration. I tore my eyes away from his and glanced beyond the guard at the king and queen standing in front of their thrones. A chill captured my skin. That man ruthlessly killed Zachary's father for his own gain. I did not want to have any part of a kingdom built on murder.

"I would like to dance a little more," I said to the guard, jutting my chin out as if that would make a difference.

Zachary smirked and looked away.

"I'm sorry, Princess. King's orders."

My prince stepped back, out of the guard's grip, and bowed, kissing my knuckles. "I will see you again, Rory," he said softly, and then disappeared into the crowd.

The guard led me up the steps to where the three thrones sat, and my father stood next to my mother with a frown on his face. Marabel, Autumn, and Felicity cowered behind him. And that vision sent my blood to the boiling point. I was not a child. If they were unhappy with my actions, they had no right to take it out on my family.

"Why is my fae family hiding behind you as if you have reprimanded them?"

The king's bushy eyebrows rose, and his face turned red. He swiped his finger toward the chair. "Sit!" he barked.

The music ground to a halt and, once again, all eyes were on me. The way Marabel, Autumn, and Felicity looked at me was just shy of visual begging. I stared the king down, ignoring their imploring eyes.

I had heard stories about the dragon queen all my life, but no one except Zachary ever told me why the queen went to such extremes. I wanted to hear my father's viewpoint on the murder. "Tell me about the dragon king."

King Henrick blanched, and his eyes widened. "Sit," he hissed.

I crossed my arms and tapped my foot impatiently. Although I was raised to respect my elders, I was not used to being ordered around. I did not like it one bit. I glanced at the queen. She did not wear a mask of anger like the king. In fact, if I had to read her expression, it looked like a barely concealed smirk. She nodded toward the seat. Her silent request was much more welcoming.

"I will sit," I mumbled and crossed to the third throne. It was decorated more for a child with hand painted animals adorning the back, rather than a future queen, but I guess that was to be expected. I settled into the seat as the king waved his hand.

Music filled the ballroom yet again.

The king settled in his seat and snapped his fingers. The suitors formed a line, and the first approached. He had greasy black hair that fell over his dark eyes, a thin, almost nonexistent mustache, and was skinnier than a twig.

"Duke of Dewimeth," a guard announced.

He bowed and then put his hand out in an invitation to dance. The way he eyed me was more as if he were sizing up livestock.

I raised an eyebrow. "No, thank you." I kept my hands folded neatly in my lap.

The queen leaned over. "Aurora, dear, you must dance."

"I was dancing." I stood, but instead of accepting the man's hand, I turned and fled into the vast network of halls. It was as if they were trying to crush my free spirit and shove it into some preconceived idea of who I was supposed to be. I blindly ran, moving as far away from the music as I could. I found a dark and quiet corner and pressed my back to the wall, trying to blend in so I wouldn't be noticed.

Hushed voices drifted in from the balcony, rising over my ragged breath. I slid closer.

"I won't be party to your madness!" a man's voice argued.

"She dies tonight, either by your hand or by the curse. You swore you would follow through. Otherwise, I would not have let you leave the safety of our sanctuary," a woman hissed.

"I will do what is necessary. Now go, before you are caught," the man snapped.

The curtains flared out at a sudden shift of air, and I caught the profile of the man as his gaze raised to the sky.

I blinked and gasped. *Zachary.* A chill skittered down my spine. Zachary's gaze snapped in my direction, and his eyes widened as they met mine.

He had been sent to kill the princess.

To kill *me.*

I spun, intending to flee, but a powerful hand grabbed my arm and pushed me into the wall face first. He covered my mouth. I glanced over my shoulder, but Zachary was not focused on me. His wide gaze was locked on the window, as if trying to shield me from whomever he had been talking to.

I tried to push him away, but he was as solid as a stone wall. I couldn't tell whose heart banged harder as he pressed against me. His heartbeat drummed against my back in a frantic beat that matched his hissing breath. A light sheen of sweat broke out on what I could see of his forehead.

My mind buzzed with questions and the longer he kept me in place, the angrier I got. Who did he think he was, handling me this way?

He cocked his head, and then twisted us around with a grip around me that was stronger than his dance pose. "Shh," he whispered in my ear, his breath hot against my skin. He led me across the room and down the hall until he found a small room with only one door. He pushed me inside, closed the door behind us, and let me go.

I turned to face him. "You were sent here to kill me?"

He mopped his face with his hand and shrugged. "I was sent to kill the princess as payback for my father. But I had no idea—"

I struck out and my open hand slammed into his cheek, silencing him. I didn't want his excuses. "The fact you came here with murder in your heart makes you no different from my father."

His hand covered the reddening skin, and he blinked at me. His mouth formed words, but every time he moved his lips, nothing came forth. He closed his eyes and leaned his back against the door, hanging his head. "Maybe I am no better than he is," he said. "I admit, I had dark intentions, but..." His eyes opened and zeroed in on me. Hunger and frustration echoed in his irises and he moved forward, pinning me to the nearest wall as his lips crushed down on mine.

I opened my mouth to protest, but his tongue darted in so fast that I froze in place at the desperation in his kiss. I shoved him away.

"No!" I pointed my finger at him. "You lost that right. You chose hate, and I cannot..." I pressed my lips together as a sheen of tears blurred my vision. "I cannot be with someone so intent on taking a life."

"I'm a dragon. I take life all the time." His tone hardened as he crossed his arms and stepped back.

His words struck deep inside me, and I recoiled. "You... you kill for sport?"

His gaze moved away from me, and his jaw tightened. He shook his head. "No." He breathed the word as if it were a curse. "*I* don't."

The chill that captured me thawed when he looked back at me. But I wasn't fooled into melting into his arms.

"So, what does 'I will do what is necessary' mean?" I jutted my chin out in defiance. If he was entertaining trying to kill me, dragon or no dragon, he would have a fight on his hands.

His lips pressed together, and he shook his head, raking both hands through his hair. "I don't know. I didn't want my mother harmed and if the king finds out she is in his territory, he will have her killed. And the last thing in the world I want to do is harm you." He waved at me and turned his back, laying his forehead on the wood. "Which puts your father at the top of my target list. But if I kill him, my mother will never forgive me, and neither will you. I am in a lose-lose situation."

The anguish wrapped around his every word moved my feet and I placed my hand on his back. He didn't move at first, but when he glanced over his shoulder at me, there was a spark in his eye, as if an idea had formed.

"What?" I asked softly.

He inhaled deeply. "Our kingdoms could form an alliance." He turned toward me. "It would certainly beat being married off to one of those fools who the king assembled just for that purpose."

I stepped back and crossed my arms. This wasn't how I ever envisioned being proposed to, but the way Zachary looked at me was exactly the way I wanted to be looked at, with raw desire.

The way the duke had looked at me, along with all the others my father had gathered, was more like someone at a livestock auction. To them, I was just a thing to own. I bit my lip.

Zachary studied my face and a slow smile formed. "Marry me so I can ravage you in the poppy fields like I've dreamed of doing since I first caught your scent."

I cocked an eyebrow. All I seemed to dream about was him as well, but still. He made it sound as though he had been pining for me forever. As a prince, I'm sure he had a line of pretty women throwing themselves at him. He reached for me, and I stepped back.

His eyes sparkled in that thrilling way they had in the field earlier today. Like the predator he was, he stalked forward and took me in his arms.

"Marry me so I can kiss you like this any time I want," he whispered in a husky voice and then pressed his lips to mine, gently coaxing my lips to part.

This time, I melted into him. The kiss brought a soft moan to his lips, as if he could never get enough of this, even if we were together for a thousand years. My entire body tingled with desire, and my arms ensnared him as I deepened the kiss.

He broke away. "Is that a yes?" Hope shined bright in his eyes.

The door banged open.

"Release my daughter at once!" the king growled from behind us.

SPINDLE Chapter 7

TWO BRAWNY-LOOKING GUARDS HELD me in place while other bigger and meaner-looking guards searched Zachary. The tip of my father's sword pressed against his neck as the guards tossed each hidden blade out of reach. Zachary had enough weapons on him to wage a one-man war.

When they finished the search, they forced him to his knees, and my father withdrew his sword, sheathed it, and glared at the two of us. He glanced at the array of sharp cutlery and his nostrils flared. He kicked the knives to the far side of the room with a grumble and started pacing.

No one knew what Zachary was.

No one knew he was more deadly than all those weapons combined.

And if they did, he would not live through the night.

Zachary remained still under the inspection, but I could tell a storm was brewing inside him. He kept his head low, but the muscles in his jaw jumped every so often, as though he were grinding his teeth. His cheeks remained flush, but he refused to look at my father as the man paced the room, muttering under his breath like a crazy lunatic.

The fae were escorted into the room, and King Henrick turned toward them, pointing an accusing finger.

"What have you been teaching her out in those woods?" he bellowed. "I found her with this... this heathen in the pantry."

"Do not yell at my family." I tried to yank out of the guard's grip, but they held fast. If the fae got close enough, they would smell the dragon blood, just as they had when they found me after my adventure in the Dragon Realm.

Zachary glanced at me. His eyes had changed enough for me to fear he was close to losing control. If Zachary shifted, he was likely to be struck down before he could do any damage.

The fae stopped short and sniffed the air. Their eyes widened, and they seemed to huddle together as their gaze shot to Zachary and then to me. It wasn't my father's overbearing growl that shocked them.

"He's a—"

My heart lurched. "My boyfriend," I blurted. "I met him near the fields on the outskirts of the enchanted forest. He's a farm boy."

All three of the fae tilted their heads like lost puppies.

"Farm boys don't dance like he does." My father pointed an accusatory finger at Zachary. "Who are you?"

Time slowed as Zachary looked up. His eyes shimmered, giving away his heritage. I twisted out of the guard's grip as my father's face went ashen. His eyes widened for a fraction of a second and then narrowed with malice. He reached for his sword.

"I'm the son of the king you killed," Zachary declared in a low and menacing voice.

My father's intent was written in the scowl on his face and his roar. All I could envision was my father's sword slicing Zachary's head clean off. I reacted, throwing myself between the two men despite the peril.

My father didn't swing his sword in an arc like I imagined. If he had, he could have easily stopped before the damage was done. No, he lunged as if fencing, and the tip of his sword pierced my chest. Agony seared my entire body, and I screamed before my lungs closed. The blade retracted, and I glanced at the shock on my father's face before I crumpled to the ground.

"No!" Zachary yelled and threw the guards off him with a guttural growl. He pulled me into his arms, cradling me as if I were the most precious thing in the world to him.

My father stepped closer.

"You old fool! Don't you think you've done enough?" he snapped at my father and then focused on me as everyone else in the room started bickering with one another.

All the noise drowned into one high-pitched buzz. I couldn't draw a breath. Hot tears slid from my eyes as I coughed. Red dots splattered on Zachary's tunic.

"Hold on, Rory," he whispered, and then pushed up his sleeve, exposing his arm. He put the soft flesh to his lips and dragon fangs appeared as he ripped his wrist wide open. He held his hand over me, and blood flowed from his torn skin right into my wound. "Please, just hold on," he said as his sharp teeth disappeared again.

His blood mingled with mine and the minute it seeped into the sword wound, I bellowed my pain in a high, gurgling cry. My body wanted away from the scalding dragon blood, but I knew what this burning agony meant. I arched into it and kept eye contact with Zachary.

My father must have known, too, because he called off the guards, ordering them to move away from us. Even the fae were relegated to the far side of the room.

Even knowing that he was healing me, concern reflected in Zachary's eyes. It wrapped around my heart even more than his blissful kiss had. I panted until my body realized the foreign substance mingling with my blood was not harmful. Pain gave way to tingling, as though I were just waking from a long sleep and I sagged in Zachary's arms.

The fae stepped closer to us.

Relief made me dizzy, but as I blinked away the wooziness, the paleness in Zachary's cheeks gave me a rush of adrenaline.

How much blood had he lost?

My gaze shot to his hand. Blood still flowed from his wound. It wasn't like his dragon form that had healed just as quickly as my wounds had. He was in mortal danger. Marabel was close enough for me to reach out and grab her silk scarf. I wrapped the fabric around his shredded wrist and met his tired gaze.

"Thank you," I said.

His lips twitched into a ghost of a smile, and then he leaned into me. I held his wrist tight as hot panic flushed my skin. He couldn't die. Not now. Not after saving my life.

"I'm okay." I palmed his cheek. "You can heal yourself now."

He smiled weakly. "I need some food and a nap," he whispered and slumped on the ground next to me.

"Throw him in the dungeon," my father barked and swiped his sword from the ground, sheathing it and sending me a hard expression.

The guards reached for Zachary, and I covered him, glaring at them. "Do not touch him," I snarled like a rabid dog. We were both covered in blood, and I glanced at my father. "I swear, I will strike you down if you try to harm him again."

"Put them both in the dungeon," he amended his order.

This time, I didn't struggle in the guard's grip. Instead, I walked close to the men hauling Zachary's nearly unconscious form away. As they carted us out of the room, my father's glare landed on the fae.

SPINDLE Chapter 8

THE GUARDS DRAGGED ZACHARY into the cell and held me in place on the opposite side as they fitted restraints around both wrists, not bothering to remove the scarf I had wrapped around his open wound. He sagged in the shackles as they snapped a metal collar around his neck and attached it to the wall with a thin chain.

"Bastards," I snapped and tried to get loose from their grip. Zachary needed food. He needed water. He needed sleep. Otherwise, he would die in this dank dungeon.

Zachary didn't react. In fact, I wasn't sure he was even breathing. His skin had gone nearly ashen. My heart drummed in my chest as they dragged a cot in for me and set it on the opposite wall. I expected chains as well, but when they pushed me down onto the thin bed and stepped away, my mouth dropped open. At least they hadn't put us in separate cells. That would have been the last straw for me. I would never forgive my father if Zachary died.

"Please, can we have some food and water?" I asked before the iron door could be slammed closed.

The guard hesitated and then gave me a nod. He disappeared, and the door clanged with such finality that I shivered. I stared at our dismal surroundings and rubbed my arms. I stood and stepped toward Zachary, but the echo of footsteps getting closer diverted my attention.

A small door at the floor opened and a metal tray with bread and a tin cup of water sat on it.

"Thank you." I retrieved the food. I headed toward Zachary, and halfway across the room, I hit an invisible barrier. The water cup fell off the tray. Fortunately, I caught the bread between the tray and my body. Unfortunately, the bread was now partly soaked with blood.

I couldn't get to Zachary to feed him or give him a drink. I tilted my head back and let out a scream that echoed throughout the dungeon. Shrill and full of anger, I threw the tray across the room. It banged the wall near Zachary.

Zachary jerked his eyes open and blinked at the surroundings. His gaze fell on his wrists and then his fingers barely brushed against the metal on his neck. "Fuck," he whispered in a hoarsely weak voice and straightened so his weight was on his feet and not supported by the chains. He winced. Blood still slowly dripped from his fingers. When he finished inspecting his situation, his gaze landed on me and drifted down to the bread in my hand.

"May I have some?" he asked.

I stared at the tray now on his side of the invisible barrier. "Think you can catch?"

He cocked his head, but he did nod and opened his good hand.

I stepped back enough so my tossing arm wouldn't hit the barrier and lobbed the bread. It hit the barrier and bounced back at me. Fury welled up inside me, tainting my vision with a red hue. I threw myself into the invisible wall and pounded on it, intending to break through with sheer force until exhaustion collapsed me on the floor.

The door creaked open. King Henrick stood just outside the entrance with his arms crossed and a scowl framing his lips.

"What have you done to my daughter?" he demanded of Zachary.

Zachary stood tall and flipped his hair back. "I have not *done* a thing to your daughter."

My father's fists clenched.

"Why did you lock us in here like this? He needs food and sleep." I waved toward Zachary.

"He wants you to watch me die," Zachary answered before my father could. His voice sounded much stronger than it had when he woke from his stupor, but his face was still deathly pale and dark circles had formed under his eyes. Blood still dripped from his wrist.

I gasped and snapped my head in my father's direction.

"He came to kill you," my father replied, to my incredulous glare.

"I know. But he didn't know *I* was *your* daughter until tonight. Besides, if he wanted me to die, he would have let me bleed out in your chambers. He didn't have to save me. He could have just as easily shifted and torched the room, too. But he didn't. What does that say about him?" My hands shot to my hips. "To me, that says he is a man of honor, even if every fiber of him wants to kill you for murdering his father." I pointed at my father. "He is a better man than you ever were."

My words seemed to defuse my father's anger.

"Why didn't you just ask my father for his blood?" Zachary blurted.

King Henrick ran his hand down his face and took a deep breath. "It wasn't enough to save them," he answered and looked at me before he crossed his arms and glanced at Zachary.

The slow meaning of his words hit me. "You... asked?"

My father pressed his lips together and nodded. "I did what I had to do."

"My father refused?" Zachary asked, with wide, unbelieving eyes.

The king shook his head. "No. He did not refuse, but it was not enough. When he stopped, I made a choice. A choice that brings us here today on the eve of my daughter's twentieth birthday. The night your mother's curse is set to come true. And here you are, with enough weapons to take down the entire royal family."

Zachary leaned back against the wall and tilted his head. "I will not harm Rory." He met my gaze.

"Her name is Princess Aurora. And I would be a fool to believe you." He glanced at me. "You should heed my warning. Until the sun shines through that window, neither of you are leaving this cell. And if he dies in the meantime, that is not my concern."

"I will never forgive you if he dies," I yelled.

111

My father scoffed at me and turned back to Zachary. "That is a very special collar. If you attempt to shift, it will break the inner seal and rows of deadly belladonna-coated blades set in the outer collar will pierce your neck. If the blades don't kill you, the poison will."

The cell door slammed, and my heart dropped into despair.

SPINDLE Chapter 9

HOW MANY HOURS UNTIL sunrise?

My chains rattled as I shivered from more than just blood loss. It was damn cold in this cell. At least the cold seemed to slow my bleeding. Even so, I couldn't do a damn thing in human form. And the deadly collar around my neck kept me from shifting and fixing this entire situation. With no food, and no way to rest chained this way, I didn't have much of a chance of making it through the night.

My brain kept circling around what Rory's father had said. *Them.* He had said my father tried to save them, but it wasn't enough. I glanced at Rory, and a lump formed in my throat at the dichotomy of emotions assaulting my already weak form. Hate for her father for taking away mine, and gratitude at what he had done because my father's death had made Rory possible.

I glanced up at the window, wishing for a miracle.

At least we weren't totally drenched in darkness. Moonlight lit up the cell enough for me to see Rory's frantic agony, and it surpassed my own.

She clawed at the invisible wall until red streaks marred the air from her bloodied fingers. Seeing her near hysteria hurt more than the cramps in my muscles. She collapsed, sobbing, and all I wanted to do was break these chains and hold her until she stopped crying.

"It's okay," I said, even though I knew it wasn't. I would never feel her body against mine or the flutter of her heart as I kissed her. Just thinking about her lips made my cock twitch.

She looked up at me and her eyes held a devastation I didn't know how to fix. She shook her head slowly as tears glistened in the moonlight. "Seeing you suffer will never be okay." Her soft voice cracked.

"I should have..." I closed my eyes and all the opportunities that I had to make her mine passed before my eyes. "I should have just taken you this morning. Damn the consequences." I leaned my head back as far as my collar would allow. I inhaled her scent, letting it wrap around me like a soft caress.

She sniffled. "I wish you had, too."

I opened my eyes and looked at her. Regret was a beast more savage than my dragon side. This was not the last emotion I wanted to experience and yet it layered over every breath, every thought. "At least I got to dance with you." I tried on a smile just for her.

It must have been more natural than I thought because her lips curved into her soft, secret smile, and damned if that expression didn't move something deep within me. I was serious in the closet when I suggested we marry, but it had nothing to do with uniting the kingdoms. It was a purely selfish want. But the odds of that happening now were not in my favor.

Somewhere, church bells started their midnight toll. She glanced out the window, and I followed her gaze, allowing a smidgen of hope to find its way into my soul. It was crushed the moment I looked back at Rory.

Her smile slowly disappeared as her eyes glazed over like someone under a spell. I should know. I had dabbled from time to time in control spells. And she certainly represented the slackening faces of my victims. My heart dropped to the floor.

"Rory?" I asked.

She showed no signs of hearing me. She stood like a marionette and took a stunted step forward. There was nowhere to go, but that did not stop my pulse from racing, creating hot pain in my wrist as the cut reopened from the newly created force of blood.

"Aurora!" I yelled, struggling against the restraints.

No response. She took another step toward the door and, like the magic that had gripped her, the door swung open on its own accord. It had to be that damn curse of my mother's.

"Rory! No!" I bellowed and watched helplessly as she walked out the door.

I yanked the chains holding me in place and let out a cry that I was certain would alert the guards. But no one came. I realized the wall that kept

Rory from me also muted my calls for help.

Still, I ranted until my voice failed and I slumped against the wall. "God damn it, Mother. Why?" I knew her reasoning. She had explained the glory of her revenge daily, poisoning my mind against humans since the day my father died.

"Fuck," I muttered, and considered shifting. I didn't have much to live for if Rory died. But if I took that route, there would be zero chance of saving Rory from my mother's grim curse. I banged my head against the wall, inhaling the last of Rory's lingering scent.

The air changed, like the days of the black death, when the wind shifted to bring the stench of rot to the other side of the wall. I had gagged on it then and I gagged on it now, coughing and spitting, so it didn't take me along for the death ride.

But this was worse. It wasn't just a random disease taking life. This was far more evil. It meant Rory was now in the grasp of my mother's curse.

SPINDLE Chapter 10

"WHAT HAVE YOU DONE?" the king's voice bellowed, pulling me from my own near-death stupor.

I rolled my head toward him. "If you hadn't chained me to the wall, I could have stopped her." Even my voice sounded defeated.

He marched across the floor and rattled keys on a round holder, looking for a specific one to unlock the clasps at my wrists. He didn't release the collar. Instead, he unclipped the end of the chain from the wall and dragged me from the room. My muscles seized and I dropped to my knees. But the king didn't show an ounce of sympathy. He just kept dragging me across the floor until I found my footing and stumbled after him like an obedient dog.

When he pulled me into the ballroom, I stopped short at the sight of so many bodies. They looked as if they had dropped in place and they smelled like death. The entire palace seemed to be in the throes of the curse. The king yanked me forward and pointed at his wife.

"Fix this!" he demanded.

I blinked at him, and my eyebrows rose. I had as much power over this as he did.

I scanned the bodies, looking for Rory. I needed to find her. I needed to know whether she was alive or whether my mother had indeed killed her. "Where is Rory?" I turned back to the king.

He pulled out his sword and pointed it at me. "Fix this," he roared.

His eyes were wild enough for me to understand there was no reasoning with him. I opened my mouth to speak, but nothing came out. All I could do was shake my head. "How?" I finally asked.

His entire face turned red. And he lifted his sword, intending to use it. I tried to yank away, but he held the chain fast.

A dragon crashed through the palace doors, sending glass and cinderblocks flying over the unconscious, nearly dead patrons. Her timing was impeccable: the king had his sword at the ready and paused at the sight of my mother in all her fiery glory, flying across the expanse.

But what caused my eyes to widen was the limp body in her talon. I would know that shade of blonde anywhere. The dragon cackled as she tossed the body our way. I lunged to catch her, but the chain holding me in place stopped my progression. Rory's body crashed down on the platform in front of us with enough force to break bones. I turned and yanked the chain right out of the king's hands and fell to my knees by Rory's side.

My mother's talons had done just as much damage as the crashing fall. My hands hovered over her because I was too afraid to touch her and do more harm. At least she was mercifully oblivious of her fragile state, but that didn't stop the sting of my own tears. I did not have enough blood to fix this. At least not while I was in human form. And even in dragon form, I did not know if it would do any good. But I had to try, consequences be damned. Maybe my blood could reverse the damage my mother's curse had done. I would have one shot because as soon as the belladonna tainted my blood, it was no longer a viable option.

"Oh, Rory," I whispered and leaned over, pressing my lips to hers one last time. My tears dripped on her face, baptizing her with what little emotion I had left. Then I glared up at my mother. "I loved her, and your damn curse killed her!" I growled and climbed to my feet, blocking my mother from Rory's body.

My mother stared beyond me, and her face morphed into fury.

A moan yanked my attention behind me. Rory's eyes fluttered open. I could not believe what I was seeing, nor did I understand it. *If my mother cursed her to die, how the hell was she breathing?* She gasped and wheezed, and her contorted and pain-filled face told me with her current condition, she wouldn't be breathing for long.

Others stirred as well, including the queen.

The king glanced around and then back at me. "You? You're true love's kiss?" he growled in disgust.

I didn't have time to answer. My mother's roar demanded all our attention.

"Nooo!" My mother reared back. Her chest glowed with the building blaze.

It made my choice easy. She was going to blast us with her fire. None of us would survive that. I closed my eyes and forced the shift. At the same time, I raked my talons over the inside of my arm, spilling more blood than I intended, right onto Rory. She screamed in response.

I expected excruciating pain. I expected daggers to bore into my flesh. But it never came. I blinked my eyes open and glanced down. The metal collar lay at my feet. The clasp on the back of the collar had been sheared clean. I never heard the metal hit the wood. Not with Rory's cries of agony filling my ears.

I glanced over my shoulder just in time to see the raven-haired fae set up another arrow. She gave me a nod and aimed toward my mother. I spread my wings, blocking the royal family and the fae alike from my mother's wrath.

My arm still dripped blood and spreading my wings wide made me grind my teeth together. I was not healing. Even my mother noticed, and her gaze softened for a moment. But then she looked beyond me again and that insane anger that had darkened her soul returned.

I stood fast. I would protect Rory from my mother's wrath, even if it meant my end.

"Move, boy," she snarled, as smoke curled from her nose.

"No." There was no use in trying to explain to her that her killing Rory was worse than what the king did. The king's actions were born of love and desperation. Hers were born of bitterness and hatred.

"He needs to know what true loss is!" she screeched so loud that people just coming out of their stupors covered their ears.

"Someday he will. But today is not that day. He did not kill Father out of anger or hatred. He made a shitty choice out of desperation. But his reasoning was more noble than yours. You want to kill for spite. He was just trying to save the woman he loved. I don't condone it, but I understand it."

"He has poisoned your mind."

"You are the one who poisoned my mind. My entire childhood was filled with lies," I bellowed at her. She had always told me humans weren't to be trusted. They should be killed on sight. Luckily, very few slipped through the walls built around our land. But I had blood on my hands, too.

"Move or you will perish with them!"

I clenched my jaw. "So be it." I refused to budge. "But know this. When you finally calm down and look around at the needless destruction you caused, it will not relieve you of your hatred. It will not bring Father back. And you will have destroyed the last piece of him you have left." I swallowed hard and steeled myself for her fire.

Rory fell silent behind me, but I couldn't look to see whether the sudden hush was from the healing or whether my blood was not enough and she had perished. I could feel the weight of that on my already taxed heart.

"Please don't hurt him." Her small voice welled up from behind me as she slithered between my wing and my torso. Tears of relief blinded me. My blood had done enough to help her walk, but she still looked as though she had kissed death. She stood in front of me with her arms spread wide as if she could withstand the dragon flames if my mother let loose.

"Rory, get back," I said softly.

She looked up over her shoulder at me with tired eyes and shook her head.

I wrapped my wing around her carefully, trying not to wince from the blood still flowing from my torn flesh.

The movement created a spiral of agony through my entire limb and I winced, losing connection with my dragon form. The shift back to human form was immediate, and I sagged under the weight of it, dragging Rory to her knees along with me. The slam into the floor ripped a groan from my chest. I pulled Rory closer so I wouldn't fully collapse on the ground.

My mother stared at us, blinking with her dragon maw hanging open. I don't think she understood the direness of my situation until that moment, and it shocked her motherly instincts back into her. At least for the moment. With her, I never really knew whether it would hold or whether she would turn back into that bitter widow again.

"Zachary?" she asked with a healthy dose of concern. She took a tentative step toward us, careful not to step on any of the humans scrambling out of her way.

I put my hand out to stop her and blood still dripped from my wrist. "She is my heart. Please don't..."

"You're... you're hurt," she gasped.

I bit my tongue on my initial reaction and just nodded. I didn't think she would appreciate sarcasm right now.

"What did they do to you?" Her voice hardened.

"Nothing. It was my choice. Rory jumped in front of a sword meant for me. I couldn't let her die." I glared up at my mother. "But because of your damn curse, we were locked up in a cell where I couldn't get the food or rest I needed to heal." I shook the creeping cobwebs from my head. "This is all because of your damn hatred." The world spun around me, but I grimly held fast.

She crept closer until she was within swatting distance. All around us, swords had been unsheathed and were directed at her. Archers had arrows ready to sail, but the king had his hand up, holding them all from attacking. I didn't think he would attack. Not while Rory was still in my grasp. But my mother had been willing to kill her own son just moments before, so maybe King Henrick would sacrifice his only daughter, too.

My mother raked her sharp teeth over the palm of her talon and hurled a giant blood ball at us.

"Hold!" the king bellowed.

Her aim was impeccable. Her blood hit us with enough force to knock us on our back. It covered us from head to toe, seeping into my mouth and my wounds while stealing my breath from my chest. Rory whined against me. I clenched my fists and clamped my eyes closed as my mother's blood healed me from the outside in, seizing every muscle.

"Damn it, I said hold!" the king yelled above my own panting breaths. The ground quaked with footsteps, but I could not open my eyes.

The wounds in my arm and my wrist stitched up in a symphony of raw agony.

When the pain faded, my heartbeat returned to my normal healthy rate and my muscles relaxed enough for me to draw a big breath. Now I knew exactly how Rory felt when I first doused her acid-burned feet with my blood. I glanced at Rory and was rewarded with a light coat of sweat on her forehead and rosy, healthy cheeks. Even her eyes looked bright, and her lips formed a small smile that shot straight to my soul.

I glanced back toward my mother, expecting to see her concerned look as we finished the painful healing process. Instead, her dragon form lay prone across the ballroom floor with at least a dozen arrows sticking out of her chest. Blood oozed from her mouth and her eyes had already taken on the glossincss of the dead.

I sat up and a wave of dizziness almost dragged me back down. Rory sat up next to me and gasped.

"Oh, Zachary." She placed her hand on my arm.

The warmth of it did nothing to quell the building anguish. Blame formed in my mind, but I squashed it. Rory certainly wasn't to blame for my mother's actions.

My gaze landed on the king as he rushed toward the fallen dragon. Fury encompassed me and I clenched my fists. *If he hadn't killed my father...*

I glanced at Rory.

If he hadn't killed my father, this beautiful woman who stole my heart would not be.

Besides, her father had been shouting "Hold" while we were in the throes of healing. I could not target this unmanageable fury at him. I hung my head and captured the emotions swirling inside me, locking them away so they didn't get loose, and created the kind of devastation I was trying to dissuade my mother from doing. I did not want to end up with a dozen arrows in my heart. Nor did I want to hurt the innocent, which was everyone in this room—save two. King Henrick, who moved toward my mother's dead form, and the queen of dragons, who lay dead on the ballroom floor, were the only tainted souls here.

Rory's hand stroked my back, and her head nestled against my shoulder. I pulled her tighter against me in a quick hug, and then released her and climbed to my feet.

I crossed the room on legs that felt as if they were encased in rocks. The crowd parted, wary of me, but still they bowed in a sign of respect. Whispers of "Dragon King" reached my ears, and I nearly scoffed, but they were right. Now that my mother lay slain on the floor, that left me in charge of the Dragon Realm.

King Henrick stepped aside, giving a solemn nod. I stopped by his side and traded a glance with him.

"I'm sorry about your mother." He even sounded sincere.

"I'm sorry, too." I glanced over my shoulder at Rory. "My mother never should have taken out her anger on a child." I met his gaze and then focused on my mother. Her scales had started the dulling process, bright colors bleeding into monochrome. I laid my hand on her cheek and leaned in close.

"I wish I could remember you before my father died." My voice cracked, and I cleared my throat, reining in the crumbling walls around my emotions. "I know you wanted me to toe the line. To keep your vendetta alive. But I can't. I'm going to unite our kingdoms and hopefully bring peace to the region."

A noise near me pulled my attention away from my mother. A few men with buckets in one hand and swords in the other approached. I stared at them and furrowed my brow.

"Not now," King Henrick whispered.

I turned fully to face the king. Rory approached as well, with the same quizzical look I was sure I sported. The crowd closed in around us.

King Henrick splayed his fingers and motioned his hands in a *calm down* motion. I glanced at the buckets again and it all snapped into place. "Are you planning on harvesting her blood?"

King Henrick opened his mouth to speak and then seemed to think better of it. Instead, he just shrugged. "Dragon blood heals the sick."

"Absolutely not." Rory beat me to the punch and took a position next to me. "There will be no harvesting of dragon blood. Period." She looked right at her father. "Ever. Do you understand?"

"But she's already dead." One of the men with the buckets waved his sword towards the dragon.

"This is the queen of the Dragon Realm. Show a little respect," I snarled.

"Fine." King Henrick waved the poachers away. "What do you propose we do with her?" he asked after the men disappeared into the crowd.

"I will bring her home to our people, and we will hold a proper funeral." I glanced down at my bloody clothing. "But if I go like this, it will start a war."

SPINDLE Chapter 11

I STEPPED CLOSER TO Zachary. He looked so lost and yet so in charge, and the combination of vulnerability and strength pulled at my heartstrings.

I glanced down at my clothing and winced. I looked just as bloodied as Zachary. "We both need to clean up and we need a change of clothes." I met my father's gaze, and he nodded, snapping his fingers in the air.

Like magic, a man and girl skittered to his side.

"Take him to the guest quarters and find him something suitable to wear," King Henrick addressed the man and then waved at the girl. "This is Anna, your lady-in-waiting, and she will take you to your quarters."

Anna bowed. "My lady." She waved toward the hallway beyond the throne.

"One moment." I put up my finger while Marabel, Felicity, and Autumn came to me, doling out hugs. When Autumn wrapped her arms around me, I whispered in her ear, "Please make sure the dragon queen is not touched while we clean up. Okay?"

"No one shall touch a scale. You have my word," she said.

I peeled out of her arms and stepped to follow Anna and the man my father had charged with making sure Zachary was taken care of. The two of them walked side by side, chatting as if they knew each other. Zachary kept in step with me.

We passed by the closet we had been in earlier and the memory ignited a heat inside me that rose to my cheeks. I glanced sideways at Zachary, and his lips formed a sad smile when our eyes met.

At the end of the hallway, his man turned left, and Anna turned right. All the heat in my face faded, and a chill gripped me as I took a few steps in Anna's direction. I did not want to be away from Zachary. My heart jump-started in my chest and I stopped to turn back toward him.

He had stopped as well and turned in my direction. Neither of our guides seemed to notice we had stopped.

"I don't want to be separated from you," he said.

I nearly melted into the floor on the spot. His vulnerable admission matched my exact sentiments. I reached my hand out and nodded my head in the direction Anna went. He didn't hesitate. He crossed the distance and took my hand. Warmth radiated from the spot our skin made contact. His eyes still held a haunted sadness that made me want to wrap my arms around him and hug him until that look went away.

When we reached my room, I nearly stalled in the doorway. It was bigger than the entire cottage in the enchanted forest.

Anna gasped at the sight of Zachary standing with me. "He's not supposed to be here," she said, wide-eyed.

"I won't tell if you won't." I pulled him inside, still gawking at the room. Zachary didn't seem as impressed as I was until we stepped farther inside, and the bathing pool came into view. It was larger than the acid swamp had been, and steam rolled slowly off the water like a silent invitation.

He dropped my hand and headed toward it, ripping his clothes off as he went. As each piece of clothing dropped, more of his golden skin appeared. He was as perfect as a god, and I followed, stripping my clothing off despite Anna's faltering protests.

"Can you get us some clothes?" I asked and then I stepped into the warm pool. Zachary was already submerged under the water, surrounded by a rust-colored haze. I looked down at the water as I walked, leaving the same rust-colored trail as he did. The dried blood dissolved around me, and I dunked under as well, running my fingers through my hair to clean what I could.

I surfaced, and Zachary stared at me.

"The chill that settled into my bones in the dungeon is finally gone." He splashed water on his face, still looking like an Adonis.

I glanced away from him, afraid that I wouldn't be able to control this need to feel him inside me. A pyramid of soaps on the other side of the pool caught my attention, and I used it as a distraction from the building heat. There were several scents, from flowery, to sickly, to refreshingly citrus. I chose the latter, but before I could start scrubbing the rest of the bloodstains from my skin, Zachary snatched the soap from my hand.

I glanced over my shoulder at him as he ran the soap over my back. His touch was light, and his brow knit, as if the soap could erase the horrible memories of the last twelve hours. I closed my eyes and indulged in his gentleness.

Disappointment bloomed when he handed me the soap and moved away. I scrubbed my stomach and breasts, soaped up my hair, and then rinsed off before turning to find him sitting on the steps, looking out the window. I bit my lip at the sadness radiating from him.

His wet skin glistened and his hair dripped unchecked. I crossed and took a seat next to him, reaching out to touch his forearm. He sniffled and glanced at me. His eyes glossed over and he blinked. A single tear slipped out of the corner.

"My mother is dead."

The sorrow strangling his voice shot straight to my heart, and I squeezed his arm.

He blinked again and his lips twitched into the saddest smile I had ever seen. It wasn't until his gaze ripped from mine to scan my form that interest wiped away the devastation. When he looked back into my eyes, the same heat I had been feeling resonated.

I did not resist when he pulled me to him, and his lips crushed against mine with blissful demand. The moment was broken by a small squeak behind us. We pulled away as if touching each other burned. My gaze snapped beyond his shoulder at Anna with an armful of clothing.

I cleared my throat. "Thank you, Anna. You can leave that on the bed.

And if you would be so kind as to make sure we are not interrupted again, by anyone, even my father, I would be ever so grateful." I sent her a smile.

"I, um..."

I raised an eyebrow, and Anna stopped fidgeting. Her gaze kept bouncing to Zachary, and I couldn't blame her. He was beautiful to look at when he was dressed, but impossible to tear your gaze from dripping wet.

"Yes, m'lady." She averted her eyes. Blush painted her cheeks, and she dumped the clothing on the bed before scurrying out and closing the door behind her.

Zachary turned toward me and cocked his head. A smile toyed with his lips, and the blaze igniting in his eyes thrilled me. He stood, giving me a full view of his exceptionally chiseled form, and offered me his hand.

I took it, expecting to be taken right there on the pool steps, but he pulled me from the water and handed me the towel from the bench. He took the other towel and started drying off his body. I did the same, towel-drying my hair as I mulled over his reserved actions. It was as if he had a change of heart from earlier. As if all this pain and death had stripped him of being able to be attracted to me.

He wrapped the towel around his waist and turned. I hadn't bothered hiding my form from him and dropped the cloth on the ground, hand-combing the knots out of my hair. His chest rose with a great inhale as he scanned me from tip to toe and back.

"Damn," he whispered and met my gaze.

I stepped forward and licked my lips as I cupped his cheek. My other hand landed lightly on his chest. The pounding of his heart against my palm told me all I needed to know. I slid my hand into his wet hair and pulled him to my lips. This time, the kiss was magical enough to slow time. I stripped him of his towel and was rewarded with a low groan in his throat.

Zachary's hands gripped my cheeks as he deepened the kiss and he maneuvered me to the wall before he broke the kiss. His green eyes flared bright as he stared down into my face, searching my gaze for any doubt. "Are you sure?"

I smiled up at him. I had no doubts about this moment. "I want all of you."

His smile rivaled the heavens above, and his hands slid from my face, down my throat, to my breasts. His touch sent tendrils of heat tingling through my entire form. I reached for him, but he stepped out of range.

"Not yet," he said, and his lips followed his hands.

He gently sucked my nipples until they were so hard, I thought I'd scream. He sent a sly grin up at me as he trailed down my stomach, stopping to delve into my belly button. His hands slid to my hips as he dropped to his knees in front of me.

He drew his knuckles across my sensitive bud, and I gasped at the sensation. Zachary lifted my leg and hooked it over his shoulder, running his fingers from my knee to my core in a tease that left me breathless. When he leaned in and licked me, I ran a hand into his hair, keeping the other against the wall to maintain balance.

When he said he wanted to devour me, I never guessed that I would be so incredibly satisfied. He built me up to the breaking point and then dialed back until I was too crazed to reason with.

"Please, Zach. Please, dear God," I panted.

"Come for me," he whispered, and then went back to his masterful ministrations.

My entire body felt as if it were on fire. And when I finally came, it was a rush that nearly blinded me with its force. All I wanted was him inside me, and he obliged, standing and entering me in one motion as he wrapped my legs around his waist.

I didn't catch my breath at my body's reaction to Zachary. It was like stepping into heaven. We moved in frantic thrusts until his muscles tightened and he groaned, and another wave of heat filled me.

He panted in my ear, with his weight pinning me to the wall. We stayed that way until both of our breaths evened out. When he finally unwrapped his arms from around me and pulled away so I could see his face, the sadness had returned to his eyes.

I swallowed hard and tried on a smile.

He gently kissed me and let go of my legs, uncoupling and letting me slip to my feet. My legs couldn't hold my weight and his grip tightened as he turned and pressed his back against the wall, with me firmly pressed to his chest.

"Dear Lord, you are amazing. I could stay in this room with you forever," he said with his head back and his eyes still closed. By the time he regained normal breathing, that bliss that covered his face faded. He glanced down at me. "But I have to go bury my mother."

His words were like a cold slap of melancholy.

"Will you come back?" I asked, afraid of the answer. He had a kingdom to run now, and I was his enemy's daughter, despite what he had said in the closet before we both almost died.

He smiled and wiped my hair from my face, planting the softest of kisses. "Of course. I plan on marrying you." He gave me another peck and picked up the towel, wiping off the sweat from his chest before he crossed to inspect the clothing.

I used the towel I had discarded to clean up before I stepped next to him, mildly disappointed that he was covering up his god-like form. I pulled the dress over my head and smoothed it over my skin. This was a different gown than what I had been wearing. The midnight-blue satin was sleeker and hugged my form more than the ballgown from earlier.

I turned toward Zachary, and he was staring at me, with his hands paused on the buttons of his shirt.

"What?" I looked down at the dress. "Is this not to your liking?"

He laughed. "Oh, it is very much to my liking." He finished buttoning up his shirt. "As a matter of fact, I don't know how I am going to walk out the door with you looking like that." He pulled me close and delivered a kiss before he slipped on the dinner jacket that was left on the bed. He put on his boots and took one last look at me.

"Can I go with you?"

Zachary bit his lower lip, contemplating, and then shook his head. "It's too dangerous. My people will be angry when I bring my mother's body back."

Danger didn't bother me. Besides, he had stepped into this castle tonight, knowing the dangers. "And you coming here wasn't?"

He looked up at the ceiling and then back at me. "I'm not sure you are really seeing this from our side. Imagine if I had killed your mother and father, and then you brought me here. How would the people of your kingdom react?"

"I didn't kill your mother or your father."

He sighed and pinched the bridge of his nose. "Okay, what if my mother killed your parents, and you brought me, the offspring of the person who killed their king and queen, here?"

It finally sunk in with a cold certainty. I was the child of the people responsible for their kingdom's monarchs' deaths. I did not think the people of the Kingdom of Light would take that lightly if the tables were turned. They would think I was a traitor and string me up along with him. "Your kingdom already hates our kind."

He nodded.

My chest tightened. "I don't want to be separated from you," I whispered and met his shimmering eyes.

Zachary cupped my cheek and gave me the softest peck on the lips. "I don't want to be separated either, but I have a duty to my kingdom and some serious damage control to do before I can think about us. My mother instilled a vicious degree of hatred in every heart in the kingdom. I need to undo that before there is any hope of peace between our kingdoms."

I knew he was right, but that still didn't stop the tightening in my stomach or the tears misting my vision.

"You have work to do here as well."

I blinked and focused on his eyes. "What work?"

"Humans hunt dragons for our blood. That practice has to stop."

I couldn't argue with him. I couldn't see taking the life of a living, breathing animal just for healing properties, but I was a minority in my thoughts. People would still want the magical healing qualities and if it wasn't given, it would be hunted. People were awful that way. My thoughts zeroed in on a solution. "What if your people were willing to donate blood?"

His lips twitched into a smirk. "Out of the kindness of our hearts?" He raised a brow.

"There must be something we have that you need."

He cocked his head and studied my face. "There may be some bartering power there. In certain seasons, food is scarce, so that is a means of trade."

"We have plenty of farms." I smiled.

He laughed. "Honey, we eat meat, not rabbit food."

Heat filled my cheeks. I forgot for a moment that he was a dragon at heart. Still, it was something that our kingdom had an abundance of. However, with the dragons eating all their meat, what would the people of the kingdom live on? It was all giving me a headache, so I stepped close and hugged him tight.

"Come back to me."

"I will always come back to you, Rory." He kissed the top of my head and then peeled out of my grip. "Always." He turned and walked out of the room without so much as a glance back.

SPINDLE Chapter 12

I FOUGHT EVERY URGE to run after Zachary and beg him not to go, but he was right—I had to figure out how to heal my kingdom's hearts and minds before we could be happy together. Instead of heeding my heart, I turned to the window, taking deep breaths so I didn't cave in to my desires. The sky beyond my ornate window had just started its daily waking process. The black of night had already transitioned into that deep morning blue. Distant rays played on the horizon, rising toward the heavens like a celestial stretch. Soon, all the colors of dawn would paint the sky.

With a heavy sigh, I crossed to the mirror and gasped at my image. My hair was a knotted mess. Thankfully, there was a brush on the counter.

"May I get you anything?" Anna stuck her head in the door.

I pulled the last of the knots free and then glanced at her. "No, thank you."

She frowned as though I had robbed her.

I sent her a warm smile to soothe her obvious unease. "I'm sorry, but I have never had a lady-in-waiting. I don't know how this works."

The furrows in her brow smoothed out. "I am here to help with anything you may need."

This was going to take a tremendous effort to get used to. Having a servant was almost as uncomfortable as the grandness of this castle when so many impoverished people were in such proximity.

"Why don't you go enjoy what's left of the food? I will be out in a moment."

"Thank you, m'lady," she said and curtsied before she ran out of the room.

I sighed at my image and set the brush down in its place before I headed back to the ballroom. I didn't want to stay here with all that had happened. I just wanted to be at our cozy cottage, which was closer to Zachary than this cold castle.

Both Zachary and I almost died, and the undertone of doom still hung in the air.

I came around the corner just in time to glimpse Zachary flying out of the palace with the limp corpse of his mother gripped in his talons. He was magnificent in dragon form, and the farther away he flew, the more his coloring blended with the breaking dawn.

My gaze dropped to the dance floor littered with those who had been crushed by the dragon when she fell. My stomach did a slow roll at the carnage, and I swallowed the burn of bile.

Musicians had already packed up and left, along with most of the guests. All that remained were my fae family, the king's guards, and the castle staff. The latter two were attempting to clean up the mess. Neither the king nor the queen was still in the ballroom.

Felicity turned toward me, as if she sensed my presence. She nudged Autumn and Marabel before she sauntered over to me with a solemn expression. As she came closer, she tilted her head and looked me over as if something had changed. Marabel and Autumn came up behind her, wearing the same curious expression as Felicity.

I shifted under their stares, but when they stepped in for a hug, I gladly accepted the warmth of their love. If I couldn't be with Zachary right now, all I wanted was to be back in my warm bedroom in the forest. But I knew that was impossible.

Anna scurried over to my side. "Can I get you anything, m'lady?" she asked while wringing her hands. Her gaze kept going to the dead strewn over the floor.

I pulled out of the hug with the fae. "Is there anything you can do to help?" I waved at the bodies.

"We cannot bring them back to life," Marabel said with a voice so filled with sadness that my throat tightened in response.

"I know. But can you help clean up? Maybe move the bodies to wherever they can be viewed or turn them into dust that the families can save. Or better yet, crystals that could be kept in their homes?"

The three fae looked at one another and then closed their eyes. Magic swelled in the air and a small tornado captured each body, turning it to ash before it reformed in the shape of a beautiful vase of flowers. Each vase was etched with the deceased's name, and different vibrant colors captured their essence.

People gasped and then clapped through their tears as their loved ones became something lovely and bright.

I knew they were strong, but I never guessed how powerful they really were. I should have known when I woke up from the curse. The dragon queen had cursed me to die along with the entire kingdom, and the fae made it so we all just fell asleep in a deathlike state who true love's kiss could undo.

I blinked, and my gaze shot out to the horizon where Zachary went. I knew there was something between us, but it never dawned on me he was the one that the fae had prophesied. I glanced at them. "Did you create the bond between Zachary and me with your magic?"

Their mouths popped open, and their eyes widened. "The dragon prince?" they asked in unison.

I nodded. "Yes. The dragon prince. Was that your doing?" I pointed at them.

They adamantly shook their heads. "No. We just wished for true love's kiss to banish the curse."

I believed them and headed for the throne pedestal. I took a seat on the stairs as the entirety of all that had happened last night pummeled my muscles. The castle staff still rushed around to clean up the rest of the mess, but at least they weren't transporting corpses off the dance floor.

Marabel, Autumn, and Felicity sat next to me on the stairs and we silently watched until most of the activity dwindled to just a few people tidying up the last of the remnants of the ball. The sun was high enough in the sky to highlight the gold and silver accents in the ballroom.

I looked up and the mural on the ceiling captured all of my exhausted attention. I laid back on the steps to get a better view and nearly laughed out loud. It was almost comical to see a mural with humans and dragons living side by side on the ceiling of the castle of the Kingdom of Light. I wondered how many times my father looked up at that ancient mural and cringed. After all, he had been the one to cause the last twenty years of hostilities.

"The dragon prince?" Autumn asked after the last of the staff had left the room, pulling me out of my thoughts.

I shrugged and my cheeks heated as I sat back up. "Yeah." I couldn't meet their inquiring gazes.

"There have been rumors that he is a cruel, cruel prince." Autumn crossed her arms.

I scoffed at her. Of course, the rumors would paint the royal dragon family as horrible, but with the wall, there really wasn't any viable source of information beyond speculation. "Does anyone have proof of that?" I glanced at each of them. They all slowly shook their heads but opened their mouths to speak. I put my hand up to stop whatever further arguments they were about to launch. "He saved my life. End of story."

I let out a heavy sigh and stared at the giant hole the dragon queen had carved in the castle wall.

"Do you think..." I waved to the destruction.

"We need some rest before we do another large spell," Felicity said.

I gave them a tired smile. "Well, if that's the last casualty of the night, we should count our blessings."

SPINDLE-A FRACTURED FAIRY TALE

SPINDLE Chapter 13

MY HOPEFUL THOUGHTS WENT straight to hell a few minutes later, when a rider on horseback barreled into the castle through the wall. He drew the horse to a stop a few feet away from us. Both he and his steed had wild eyes, as if they had seen the start of a bloody war.

"The barrier is gone, and dragons are burning the fields!" he whispered with a ragged voice and then fell off the horse, landing at my feet. His entire back was singed and bloodied. I glanced at the horse and what I had thought were streaks of mud was actually the young rider's blood. He had ridden all this way to warn us of the chaos at the far side of the kingdom.

I moved to his side, but there was nothing I could do. His injuries, along with the hard ride, had taken everything from him. A lump formed in my throat at the senseless loss, and I glared at the opening. I had to stop them before anyone else was harmed.

I didn't even turn back toward the fae. Instead, I jumped on the horse's back and slammed my heels into his side. He took off as if dragons were chasing him again and I steered him out of the castle doors.

The fae called after me, but I needed to stop any escalation in hostilities before it got to the point my father retaliated.

I drove the horse faster and held tight to the reins. My heart pounded in my chest and my mouth dried of all spit at the plumes of smoke in the distance. It took hours to reach the farmlands, and the sun had not been kind on my exposed skin, but I didn't care. I only had one thought circling in my mind: *protect the innocent souls.*

I drove the poor horse beyond normal limits and the beast complied, seeming to understand the urgency of the situation. When I rode past a huddled group of farmers toward the terror in the skies, they screamed for me to hide, but I ignored them. I passed several dozen people and every one of them oozed fear at the flying flame machines wreaking havoc all around them.

I kept going almost to the line of blackened soil and stopped. I climbed onto my feet on the horse's back and held my hands up, screaming "Stop" like I had the authority to make the dragons cease their warlike behavior.

I did not think this through at all. These were not like the creatures in the enchanted forest that would stop and listen to me and do as I said.

Talons wrapped around my waist and yanked me into the air. I struggled in the grip as the dragon brought me higher into the sky. High enough to see bodies broken in the fields below. This was their game, and I was now at their mercy.

Even knowing that my life could end just like those below, I kicked and screamed, clawing at whatever purchase I could get on the dragon's talon. I would not go quietly, and I certainly was going to draw blood, too, if I could.

The dragon tossed me into the air, laughing as he did so.

"Asshole!" I screamed at him. Another talon snatched me out of the air, jerking me to a stop. I punched at his grip around me.

"None of those fools even thought to fight us." He chuckled ruthlessly. "You are either incredibly brave or incredibly stupid."

"You are an idiot!" I snarled and reached behind me to claw at the talon with my own fingernails. The talon tightened, and I cried out at the pressure.

"She's a pistol." The dragon tossed me to another dragon as if I were nothing more than a toy.

Each impact jerked the air from my lungs. However, they were flying away from the fields and the innocents below. Somehow, I had diverted their attention enough to stop the destruction. Although the volume of land blackened—along with the number of bodies strewn in the fields—made me fear the consequences.

I got a clear view of the Dragon Realm between my jaunts of fighting and being tossed from one dragon to the next. At least their talons hadn't pierced my skin, but I was going to have some serious bruises. My entire body ached, but I still fought. Their lewd comments sent a chill of dread through me. If they got their way, I would be their chained concubine until they tired of me and ended my life. And my death was described in horrifying detail.

My breath caught in my throat as I was tossed yet again. This time, I hit stone and tumbled across a rocky floor until I hit a wall hard enough to make me see stars. Rough hands grabbed me, yanking me to my feet. Two men with the same glittering eyes as the dragons who snatched me off the horse pulled me farther into a large interior cavern filled with people who didn't even give me more than a cursory look before they continued mining rocks from the walls with scrapped and bloody fingers. Each person looked half-starved and their exposed skin sported bruises. Every single person was also branded with a dragon symbol.

The men dragged me toward a fire pit with half a dozen brands glowing red. I renewed my struggle, breaking free from the two thugs. I bolted through the entrance and skidded to a stop when four men turned toward me. Their eyes shimmered with interest.

"Spitfire," one said, and I recognized the voice. My heart dropped just before a body tackled me from behind.

"This one needs to be tamed. Chain her in here," the biggest man said. He was the one I had called an asshole.

I struggled in the man's grip, even after my right wrist disappeared under the bite of a shackle anchored into the right wall. I pulled my left arm against my chest, resisting the guard as he tried to yank it free. The others gathered close and the largest man held another shackle out for my arm. The clasp pinched as they slapped it on and stepped back, huffing just as much as I was.

I snarled and yanked, but it was futile. When the men got within kicking distance, I lashed out, connecting with one of their shins. That earned me a slap across my cheek. Heat bloomed where his hand connected, and I glared at him, blinking away the stinging tears.

"I promise you will pay for this," I said.

They laughed at me and when I kicked out again, one grabbed my leg and put a leg restraint around my ankle. I kicked my free leg and was rewarded with a grunt. I smirked until they forced that leg into a fourth shackle.

I was totally screwed, and fear finally showed itself as trembling. These were not merciful beings. Their minds had been poisoned by their queen, and some war pact seemed to have been started at her death. The barrier between our kingdoms had perished with her, and now her people were hell bent on destroying the Kingdom of Light.

I knew if I revealed I was the lost princess, my chances of survival would diminish. But I also had heard their vile banter in the skies as they carried me here. Their version of taming me into submission aligned with the complete helplessness of my current state. I had no defense against anything they wanted to do to me, and the spark of interest in their eyes made my blood run cold.

Footsteps approached from behind. One man reached a sharp claw out and tore the shoulder hem of my dress, exposing my right breast and my back. Then he grabbed my hair in his fist and pulled my head forward. I struggled against his grip, but there was nothing I could do.

He stood close enough for me to see the outline in his pants. His free hand reached out and pinched my breast. For a moment, nothing registered and then the smell of burning flesh reached my nostrils. My body reacted, arching away from the source of pain burning my shoulder, and I screamed. The man holding my hair pressed against me, and I guess he decided branding me and pinching my breast wasn't enough of a punishment for interrupting their fun in the fields. His clawed fingers dug into my skin and his breath quickened in my ear.

I pulled away from him and the burning brand bit deeper into my shoulder. I gagged on bile and swallowed between cries. The others laughed at my reaction.

Metal banged on the floor behind me. "You are our slave now," the man who scarred me whispered in my ear. His claw raked down my back, shredding the silk dress along with my skin.

I tried to pull away, but that pushed me into the bastard standing in front of me. My hair was released and the man in front of me stepped away, yanking his nails from my skin.

The man behind me sniffed the air around me, and a low growl formed in his throat.

"You smell like dragon blood."

My heart thundered at the accusation filling his voice.

"You killed our queen," he said.

"No," I whispered through the debilitating pain. But it wasn't convincing, not when every muscle in my back was singing with acute agony and the man in front of me was reaching for his pants. His expression had changed from interest to one so full of hatred that I shivered.

The man behind me grabbed a handful of hair and yanked my head back, forcing me to look into his feral face. "I'm sure the prince will want to have a word with you once he is done grieving. Until then, we will see what kind of spitfire you really are."

When he released my hair, I slammed my head back, right into his nose. The connection left me dizzy. "Perhaps you should get your prince before you sign your own death warrant," I said through gritted teeth.

A hand came from behind and gripped my neck so tight I could barely breathe. "If I had my way, I'd mount you and shift just so I could watch as I tore you apart from the inside," he growled.

Someone cleared their throat, and the men stepped back.

"The prince gets first rights," an elderly voice said from behind me. "You know this rule," he added in a chiding manner.

The two men closest to me sneered at me. One pointed. "I will get my turn with you." He turned and took flight out of the cave, along with the rest of his friends.

"Thank you," I said before the shuffle of feet got too far away.

"I wouldn't be thanking me, young lady. They may have been the more humane end, considering you reek of the queen's blood."

SPINDLE Chapter 14

I HAD NO IDEA how long I stood with my legs wide and my arms pulled almost too tightly to the sides. My shoulders ached. My back still felt as though I had been doused in hot coals despite the shivers that the icy wind blowing through the caverns created. The pool of blood below me had all but dried, even though it still felt as if hot trails worked their way down my back and legs. It was maddening, and I more than understood Zachary's pain in the dungeon.

My eyelids felt as though rocks had been tied to them. I fought to keep them open, but I was losing the battle. The jerk of my head falling forward shocked me awake again, and I blinked the sleep from my eyes. But again, the darkness beckoned.

I coughed and tried to draw a breath, or at the very least, swallow, but that was getting difficult.

Coolness met my lower lip, and I jerked away. My eyes widened at the young woman holding out a small tin cup.

"Water." Her voice was as weak as I felt.

"You will be punished for giving her water," a voice hissed from behind me.

The girl scoffed and held the cup to my lips. Cool liquid slid into my mouth, quenching the dryness. I swallowed it and drank the rest, letting it provide me with a small second wind. "Thank you," I said, meeting her gaze.

"I have never seen anyone fight the dragons before," she said with awe. "Usually they are blubbering fools who beg for mercy."

I gave her as much of a shrug as I could muster in my position. Begging wouldn't work with those men. And reasoning wouldn't work either. Dropping Zachary's name would have only done more harm to his crusade.

The woman started to go.

"How long have you been here?" I asked.

She bit her lip and glanced over my shoulder at the woman who I couldn't see. "I don't remember." She met my gaze. "Too long," she said under her breath and stepped away.

"And the prince knows about this?" I asked before she disappeared out of my range.

She pressed her lips together and nodded. "Anyone who falls into the prince's favor dies a horrific death." She scurried away, leaving me with more questions than answers.

Time stalled and the aches in my body gained traction into blinding pain that brought black spots to the edges of my vision. My knees finally gave out, but the shackles around my wrists held me fast. My head lolled forward, and my hair hung over my face.

Wind whipped through the cave. It took my muddled mind a moment to realize it wasn't wind, but the pounding of wings I heard. I wanted to raise my head, but I didn't have the energy.

The scratch of several talons filled the space, and then the sound of footsteps approached.

"This one needs breaking." A man grabbed a handful of hair, pulling my head back enough for me to see shapes before me. "If you do not want the honors, I will gladly take that role."

One figure stopped in the middle of the group of men. Someone held a torch out close enough to illuminate my face and blind me. I turned my head away from the heat.

"Let go of her." Zachary's voice was colder than the wind.

The hand holding me released my hair and my head dropped forward again. A hand cupped my cheek and raised my face. I tried to pull away, but I was too weak. I met Zachary's gaze.

"Unchain her!" His voice barreled through the room and everyone froze in place, and then people shuffled around.

Both my arms released, and I collapsed forward. Zachary caught me and lifted me off my feet. I didn't even realize my ankles had been freed until I was in Zachary's grip.

"You fools," he growled and turned away, carrying me out of the cave.

"Let the slaves go," I whispered.

Zachary looked down at me. "We will discuss that when you are better."

I found the last of my energy reserves and pushed against his chest and nearly tumbled to the ground. "Let them go. We are not at war. You should not keep humans enslaved."

He glared at me. "We will discuss this later," he said through gritted teeth.

Before I could wage another argument, he transformed and gripped me gently in his talons as he took off into the air.

"Damn it, Zach," I whispered.

The beast huffed and glanced down at me with his green eyes blazing.

Soon after his shut-up glare, I faded into the black.

WETNESS BATHED MY BACK, followed by acute agony, that knocked me back into the darkness.

I woke with a gasp and sat up in a strange bed, disoriented. A hand landed on my back and I jumped.

"It's okay." Zachary's tired voice came from next to me. "You're safe."

I glanced toward his voice and reached out, cupping his cheeks. "Did you let them go?"

Silence followed, and he pulled from my grip.

"Zachary?" I reached out and only found an empty bed. The curtains across the room pulled back, framing his form in the moonlight. He glanced back at me.

"I had a difficult time pulling the dragons back into our kingdom aftcr the thorn wall disappeared. They wanted revenge for the queen. I finally won that argument. You were another explanation that did not go over well."

He left the curtain open and crossed the room. "You were more of a fight than pulling the troops back was." He ran his hand through his hair and took a seat on the bed with his back to me. "They still don't know you are the princess, but they know you saved my life. They also know my mother saved both of us before she was killed."

"But you are imprisoning innocents," I said.

"Yes. And right now, they are safer where they are. With your disappearance, your father is bringing the fight to us." He glanced over his shoulder. "I need to know if you will stand with me."

I reached out and touched his back, running my fingers over his smooth skin. My heart squeezed. I had more of an alliance with this man than my own blood. I wished it was more of a struggle for me to choose a side, but as long as Zachary was fair and just, I would stand in his court.

"No one else dies."

Zachary met my gaze and held it for a full breath before he nodded.

"And once a peace treaty is signed, you will release those prisoners." I poked his back.

"Once we marry and peace is certain, I will release the humans." He turned my way, pulling me into his arms. When his hand brushed the back of my shoulder, I winced.

"Sorry." He kissed the top of my throbbing shoulder. "The brand didn't heal." He sighed. "I'm told it will take a while."

Fantastic. I was branded as a slave. "What will this mean to your people?" I asked, remembering the degrading way the dragons had treated me. With this brand, I might never be treated as an equal.

"You are mine."

I pulled out of his arms. "I am not something to own," I snapped and turned to get up.

He grabbed my wrist.

I yanked my arm from his grip and got out of the bed. "But I do. That says you are mine in the eyes of the public. It means you will be safe."

"You do not own me," I snarled.

He moved fast, blocking my exit before he took me in his arms. "I've coveted you since that first day I laid eyes on you. I claimed you the day I saved you from the acid pool." His eyes blazed with fire. "And I sealed that claim before I left your castle."

"I am not your slave."

He laughed and looked at the ceiling, as if asking it for some wisdom. "I never said you were, regardless of the branding on your back. When I couldn't erase it from your skin, I embellished it. You have the mark of royal blood. So yes, they will recognize you as belonging to the king."

I still wasn't convinced. Especially after what the kind slave who had given me water had said. "Is that what you did with all your slaves?"

His smile faded, and he stepped back, looking at the floor instead of me. His features held remorse. He shook his head. "Before you wandered into our kingdom, I was as brutal as my mother. I believed her lies. I believed your kingdom rejoiced in my father's death, therefore I acted brutally and without mercy."

"You... killed them for what? Sport?" He had told me he hadn't killed for sport. "Because it was fun to kill the poor human slaves?"

He bit his lip and shook his head. "It wasn't for sport. And it was far from fun. Taking a life never healed the wounds deep in my heart."

"Then why? Why would you so callously take a life?"

"I thought I was avenging my father's death by slaughtering the ones I found... attractive." He wiped his face. "I thought I was betraying my father's memory every time I had a physical reaction. So... I tore them to pieces."

I stepped back, putting distance between us. "And what about those times you saw me in the woods hunting? Why wasn't I included in your search for vengeance?"

He pressed his lips together and stared at me in silence.

"Well?" I snapped when he didn't answer.

"I was going to kill you, and then you apologized to that rabbit and sent my entire world into chaos."

I didn't know how to feel. I blinked and opened my mouth to speak, but I couldn't think of anything that resembled an appropriate response. "Those slaves were innocent."

"I know that now. Why the fuck do you think I haven't been anywhere near the mourning hall? I cannot pay my respects to a woman who made me into such a fucking monster." His voice rose as he stalked toward me.

He grabbed me and planted a violent kiss on my lips.

"You showed me the truth. You allowed me to see the goodness in humankind. You, Rory. You also showed me just how wrong I had been and how unjust I behaved." He looked around the room. "I do not deserve to be the head of a kingdom. But I have no choice, and I need you by me to keep me humble."

I stared up at him, still unsure of what to say. I did not know whether I could be with someone so callous.

"You changed me, Rory. The times I saw you hunting, I did not understand that pure souls exist, but I knew you were different, and I looked forward to getting a hint of your scent. When it didn't come for so long, I thought the same as you. I thought you were a ghost. Something I created in my mind to temper my fury." He drew his hand through his hair. "I can't lose you," he said softly. His eyes held a deep anguish for everything he had done in his past.

If he could find it in his heart to forgive my father for what he had done, and no longer saw humans as the enemy, I had to give him the benefit of the doubt despite the fact my brain could not wrap around everything he just laid on me. "I'm not property," I finally said.

"Then be my partner. Be my queen."

Before I could answer, a knock sounded on the door.

"Come," Zachary said, loud enough to be heard in the hall.

The door creaked open and I could only see the iridescent eyes of a dragon in human form in the hallway. "Sunrise is almost upon us, my lord," he said. "And the general is waiting."

SPINDLE Chapter 15

A KING'S CORONATION WAS supposed to be a celebration of passing the seat from one generation to the next, at least from all the stories Marabel told me. Yet Zachary's step onto the throne and control of the Dragon Realm was anything but. Only a few dragons stood in the throne room when we entered.

"Are you serious?" a few of the dragons standing in the shadows said in unison. They waved at me as though I were an annoying pet.

"Yes. I'm serious," Zachary snapped and looked at the general. "Can we get on with this? I have a war to stop."

The high general of the dragon force stared down at him from his perch on the throne pedestal. His ribbons and medals pinned to his uniform covered his entire right side, and the royal dragon crest covered the left. In his hand, he held the king's crown. His gaze drifted to me and then back. "This is a private affair. One that a human should not be present for." His distaste came through in the word human.

Zachary took a large inhalation. He leveled a glare at the general. "I am the last in the royal bloodline. Are you going to deny me the throne because of an unwarranted prejudice?"

Silence layered on the room, and I glanced at Zachary. He kept eye contact with the general and his calm mannerism seemed to break whatever standoff was occurring between the two.

"No," he said through clenched teeth, and then closed his eyes to gather himself. He shifted the crown to be in both hands and nodded at Zachary.

The general uttered an ancient oration in a language I did not recognize before he set the crown on Zachary's head. The moment he removed his hands, the crown ignited in a ring of flame that matched the markings of his dragon form.

My shoulder flared with pain, but I bit my lower lip, trying not to let the whimper escape. Zachary glanced down at me and then his gaze moved to my back. To the brand on my shoulder. His eyebrow cocked and then he glanced at the general and gave him a subtle nod.

The dragons in the room bent a knee to their new king. I went to do the same, but Zachary shook his head and threaded his fingers through mine.

"There will be no more attacks on the Kingdom of Light," he said.

Heads snapped up and mouths popped open for an instant, and then gazes dropped to our intertwined hands. Hardness replaced the shock on most of their faces.

"But..." the general started before he had the good sense to close his mouth.

"We went through this already when I first arrived with my mother's body. If they attack, then we have a right to defend our kingdom. However, if I *can* broker peace between the realms, then killing humans for food or any other reason beyond self-defense will become a criminal offense."

My eyebrows arched at his statement and this time, I was the one with the mouth hanging open.

"If I of all people can rise above the anger and hatred my mother sowed into me, the same hatred that brings war to our lands and threatens our people, then all those who live in our majestic kingdom should rise to the same challenge. Acting as savage beasts is beneath us. We must set an example and show our true strength. The strength of our minds. If we seek to wage war for the sake of war with the humans, we will never see an end to it. I, for one, do not wish to see that kind of destruction. I will not risk my people when there is a chance for peace standing right here before us." He glanced at me and then back at the general. "If they are unwilling to come to the table, then I will have to rethink my position."

The general sighed. "Yes, my lord." He nodded.

"Thank you. Now, on a different note. Please make sure the elders are present when I return from the border. I will marry the princess of the Kingdom of Light and putting an end to this madness."

Their gazes locked on our intertwined hands. A couple of the guards looked confused, but the others practically had steam rising from their heads. However, no one made a comment. After all, Zachary was now their king.

"Let's go stop your father before he starts a war no one wants," he said to me and transformed, with me gripped in his talon. My stomach dropped as Zachary took to the sky like a speeding arrow.

The dragon force was something to behold from my perch in the sky. Thousands of dragons soared over the land, headed toward the border, and an evident fight. Zachary flew high and then dove at a speed that terrified me. He successfully beat the pack to the border, where my father's army had assembled en masse.

My heart hammered in my chest at the sheer number of arrows pointed in our direction as Zachary landed at the front of the dragon force.

He gently set me on my feet and transformed into human form as the general landed behind him. The general spread his blue and red wings out wide, holding off the rest of the dragons. It was a spectacle to see, and the troops yielded, waiting for their orders from either the general or their king.

I turned toward my father's army, and too many weapons were aimed in Zachary's direction. All I wanted to do was jump in front of him and yell for my people to cease their hostilities.

The dragon force surrounding us could wipe out the entire human army with just one fiery breath, and that could include us if the news Zachary announced in the castle hadn't reached the front lines. I wasn't sure his people had the ability to let go of their hatred so readily.

Zachary took my hand and crossed over the dried husks of the thorn bushes that had been there a couple of days ago. I could almost feel the sting of them as they crunched under my feet. I swallowed hard at the unyielding firing line. Hundreds of arrows were aimed in our direction. The last time arrows were aimed at a dragon, she ended up dead. I did not want to see that pattern repeated today.

"Hold!" the king bellowed and came forward.

Zachary raised his hand and glanced over his shoulder. With only a hand signal, the dragons behind us relaxed and stepped back, giving us the ability to negotiate before they rained havoc on the human force.

"What are you doing with my daughter?" King Henrick growled as he came within hearing distance.

Zachary glanced at me. "Saving her life. She seemed to think she could stop the rest of the dragons in their misguided actions earlier. My apologies for their behavior. They did not have the king's blessing to launch that attack."

King Henrick blinked at Zachary and then looked at me. "Is this true?"

I kept a grip on Zachary's hand and nodded. I wished Zachary had insisted on an outfit that covered my back. I felt uncomfortable in this dress. I would rather be in my hunting pants and soft shirts that I used to wear. Having my shoulders exposed made me feel naked, but I understood it was necessary until my shoulder healed completely. At least the dress looked a bit like the one I had been wearing when I rode out of the castle before all hell broke loose.

"Thank you for keeping her safe and returning her to us." He put his hand out as if he expected me to cross and take it.

Zachary laughed. "I did not keep her safe for you. I kept her safe because before the sun sets tonight, she will be my queen. And we"—he pointed between the king and himself—"are going to sit down and figure out a reasonable peace treaty between our kingdoms. One that benefits both sides."

My father's face turned bright red and his hand went to the hilt of his sword. "Humans and dragons have never wed. I will not allow it," he snarled.

"I'm not asking, Your Highness."

Zachary's hand tightened on mine. I squeezed back to let him know I was with him and would not run away if this all went to hell. The only thing that kept my heart slamming like a galloping horse were the arrows still aimed at Zachary's chest.

"I am inviting you and your royal delegation to the peace table." Zachary layered a warning into his voice. "Or we can keep the hostilities going and wipe each other off the map."

My father's knuckles whitened on the hilt as his lips disappeared, but he did not unsheathe the sword.

"Need I remind you, my parents, the king and queen of *my* kingdom, were killed on your land? One murdered by your hand, the other an unfortunate mistake. I would be well within my rights to strike you down on the spot. But your heinous act made Rory possible." He glanced at me. "And for that, I am inclined to forgive."

His tone held a chill that made me shiver, but he was trying to put a twenty-year grudge behind him.

"Your thugs killed several innocent farmers today," King Henrick said. "That cannot be dismissed."

The dragons behind us rose to their full heights, casting shadows over us. Their aggression seemed to agitate my father's troops.

I tore my hand out of Zachary's grip and stepped between the two kings, splaying my hands to either side. "Stand down!" I shouted. "Both sides, just stand down. Go home. Hug your children and live another day. This is not worthy of more killing. Dragons are not the enemy," I said to the humans gathered, and then turned to the dragons. "And humans are not the enemy." I would not let either side flex their testosterone. "Two decades of high tensions borne of hatred cultivated by your queen does not disappear in an instant. I understand that." I spoke to the dragons. "Your kingdom has not fallen. Just as mine has not. Trust in each other needs to be rebuilt, and I believe it can with time and the right treaty in place between our kingdoms. With the right agreement in place, we can prosper at a level beyond what we have ever seen, as long as our minds are not being poisoned with hatred."

My father stared at me as if I should just shut up and be a humble daughter. But Zachary barely contained his smile. The more I spoke, the more his eyes sparkled with pride. When I finished, Zachary raised a challenging eyebrow at my father and waved the dragons away.

All but the general obeyed, retreating towards the castle. The general stayed with his king, but gave us enough room to negotiate. Even with his showing of true leadership, my father kept that level glare at Zachary.

"Come home, girl," he said to me in a stony voice.

"I am home." I stepped back by Zachary's side. "And if you decide to retaliate instead of taking the peace offering, there will be nothing anyone can do to stop the dragons from annihilating your kingdom."

"Send the fae to settle your mind on what you fear most. They have the power to see the truth. Besides, I am sure Rory would like time with them here. And then, when your fears have been eased, bring your delegation to our castle." He glanced over his shoulder at his general. "If King Henrick sends a delegation, see that they arrive safely."

"Yes, Your Highness," the general said.

Zachary looked back at King Henrick. "I assume you know the way?" His voice lilted up at the end of the sentence as if it were a question.

My father pressed his lips together and glanced at both of us before he gave Zachary a curt nod.

205

Zachary took my hand and backed up onto dragon property, transforming gracefully. He reached for me with his talon.

I swatted it away and gasps sounded from the Army of Light, as if I had committed an atrocity that was sure to have me turned into cinder in a snap. It made me suppress a smile. "No. I don't want to be carted around in a talon. If you insist on flying, I get to ride."

"As you wish." He bent down so I could climb up his wing.

I crawled up his scaly wings and settled on the back of his neck and tightened my thighs, gripping his horns to steady myself. When I looked forward, the entire force of guards had their mouths dropped open at the spectacle. Even my father looked shocked. I smiled and waved before getting my grip set.

"I'm good," I said to Zachary. When he launched into the air, I gripped tighter with both my legs and my hands. The wind whipped through my hair and I got one last look at the armies below, all staring up in awe. Zachary arched around and headed toward the castle in the distance.

Flying on his back was much more freeing than being clasped in a talon. The air surged around me as his wings lazily beat in the air. The Dragon Realm was stunning from this height, colorful and lush. It extended as far as the eye could see, or at least until the endless blue took over. I couldn't tell whether it was a body of water or the sky.

"What's that in the distance?" I asked.

"That, my dear, is the ocean," he said. "I will take you there once we get this peace treaty in place." He dove toward the castle, bringing his wings close to his body like he had done before.

Adrenaline made my skin tingle and my breath caught in the rushing air. Tears blew from the corners of my eyes, and I laughed like I did when I was a child running through the woods at top speed. This was far more exciting.

Zachary evened out and drifted on the wind until he landed softly on the ground outside the castle entrance. He bowed so I could slide off and then shifted back into human form with a smile so enchanting that my knees weakened underneath me.

He clasped my hand in his and headed inside the castle into the room that he had been coronated in earlier. Gold glistened in the sunlight, giving the room a soft hue that didn't erase the severity of the onlookers standing on the throne pedestal. A half dozen elders stood waiting for the king, along with a few of the men who had been here earlier.

As we got closer, the oldest one, with white hair and even whiter eyes, stepped forward.

"You are dishonoring your mother and father," he said with a shaky voice of the ancient.

"No. I am not. Do you know the reason my father was killed?"

"It was cold-blooded murder." Another stepped forward, not as old as the first.

"That is exactly what my mother told you, wasn't it?" Zachary asked, but his tone wasn't argumentative, like it had been with my father on the battlefield.

"Yes."

He pressed his lips together and looked down at the ground. "Were humans our enemy before my father died?" He looked up.

They all traded glances.

"Well... no," the eldest said.

"Then why must they be our enemy now?"

"Because they killed your father and mother," he said.

"My father's death was not premeditated. It was not murder in cold blood, as my mother said. Those were the words of a wife in mourning. My father was killed in a moment of desperation because King Henrick needed more blood than my father could give and survive. He killed my father to save his own wife and child." He glanced at me. "And it tore my heart apart when I found out Rory was the benefactor of my father's sacrifice." He scanned each face. "If my father had not given his life, my soulmate would have never been born. So, you see, I can forgive my father's death because of this wonderful gift."

"They killed your mother."

Zachary shook his head. "She was angry that the king's daughter survived the curse. She was angry that I chose Rory over her hatred. She was angry that I forgave my father's death." He wiped his face. "Her death was a mistake brought on by her own actions. One minute she was threatening to kill us all, and the next she healed us." He pointed between us. "She lunged forward, and the king's guards reacted, despite the king telling them to hold."

They stared at the two of us. "Why were you wounded?"

"Rory saved my life by jumping in front of her father's sword. So, I saved her life with dragon blood. You know as well as I do that using our blood while in human form has its limitations."

They exchanged glances again, all nodding at Zachary's statement.

"Rory's father put us in a dungeon. He still thought I had nefarious plans for her, and, well, I didn't fare all that well for half a night in chains. And the curse still befell her and the entire kingdom. And again, I attempted to save her."

"If she fell into your mother's curse, how is she standing here? How is the Kingdom of Light not devastated?" The elder waved a leathery hand in my direction.

He opened his mouth to speak but slowly closed it, and I realized the Dragon Realm did not know about the gift the fae gave me after the dragon queen fled my parents' castle.

"My fae guardians bestowed a last gift after your mother uttered her curse and fled. They made it possible for the darkness to be lifted by true love's kiss." I glanced at Zachary.

His eyebrows rose. He hadn't known about the fae's gift.

"Did you kiss me after the curse took hold?" I asked softly.

His eyes seemed to look through me, as if inspecting his own memories. When he focused again, he nodded. "I did. I thought you were dead. It was my way of saying goodbye." He let a little laugh escape. "Your father mumbled something about that, but I didn't pay any attention to him. I was too concerned with my mother's reaction to everyone waking up."

"Your kiss saved all of us," I whispered and squeezed his hand.

He glanced down at our clasped hands and then focused back on the elders. "I may have broken the curse, but we were far from okay. If my mother hadn't shot a blood bomb at us, we wouldn't be here," he finished and met their solemn gazes.

"You have proved that humans are still a menace." The elder crossed his arms.

"Azdok, you must let go of that notion. They are not a menace," Zachary said in exasperation. "I wish to marry Rory, with or without your blessing," he added.

"You will be stripped of your royal status if you do so."

"That is not how this works." Zachary's voice grew cold as his eyes flashed with flame. "I am the son of King James and Queen Magna. The rightful heir to the throne. I have the same magical element surging through my blood that my mother had. The same power that made you quake in your shoes any time she lost her temper. While I have only used it to breach the thicket wall in the past, do not underestimate *my* power."

The wind in the room picked up and lightning stretched across the ceiling, crackling dangerously. I had never seen anything like it. Nor had I ever experienced the raw power radiating from Zachary. The crown on his head flashed into blue flame.

The elders huddled closer together, staring at the light show Zachary seemed to produce.

I put my hand on his arm and he glanced down at me, looking more like a god than a man. Still, I did not cringe away from him. He covered his hand over mine and looked back at the elders.

"Do we have an understanding?" he asked. As if to punctuate his question, a bolt of lightning crashed down in the space between us and the elders, followed by an ominous crack of thunder.

SPINDLE Chapter 16

THE DOORS BLASTED OPEN, and both Rory and I turned. I reined in the magic and it filled my form, threatening to overtake me before I got control of it again. I blinked at the three fae marching inside the throne room. They were the same ones who had counteracted my mother's curse. A rotund, gray-haired fae, a tall, dark fae, and an auburn-haired fae all marching as if I were the enemy. Thankfully, they weren't followed by an army. I wasn't prepared for war with Rory's father, and I prayed it would never come down to that.

I glanced at Rory, and her face lit up with a smile that warmed my soul. She broke free and ran to them, doling out hugs as if they were her dearest relatives. I guess perhaps they were, considering they raised her. And they did a hell of a job. The woman had the heart of a queen and within the hour, she would be *my* queen, despite what these old fools said.

Rory drew the fae closer, but with each step along with the whispered chatter, her smile faded. She glanced at me and then at the fae who raised her.

"He does not have me under a spell," Rory said, loud enough to be heard over the murmurings of both the fae and the elders on opposite sides of the room.

Irritation spurred a rawness in my blood. Another hurdle that almost had me throwing my arms up in defeat. I drew a deep breath and turned my back on the elders, crossing to Rory's side.

If it wasn't for the fiery-haired fae, I would have been killed by the blades in the collar when I shifted. "I owe you a debt of thanks for saving me and then protecting my mother's body while we cleaned up," I said loud enough for the elders to hear. All I needed was for them to declare these fae as the enemy. I bowed my head in respect. Their combined magic radiated from them, and I recognized the ancient power I had been too preoccupied to notice back at King Henrick's castle.

"Prince Zachary, have you put a spell on Aurora?" the dark fae said. Her eyes narrowed as if she looked straight through to my soul.

"Felicity." Rory sighed in annoyance.

The dark fae glanced at her. "I need to be sure this is not some ruse manufactured by the son of the dragon queen." She waved at me.

Rory glanced at me with wide eyes. "He didn't even know who I was," she said, defending me.

"Rory is right. I did not know she was King Henrick's daughter when I saved her from the acid lake," I said. "Her scent caught my attention years ago, and her beauty stole my heart."

The older fae put her hand over her heart, as if I had reached in and touched her with my words. But the one with the flaming hair rolled her eyes. Rory joined her, but at least she had a smirk.

"I opened the thorn wall for her to leave our land," I added, and their smiles faded. "I possess the magic to do as you suggest, but I have never used it to manipulate her mind. That is low, even for me."

The redhead crossed her arms, as did the raven-haired fae. The one with gray hair seemed to be just as enamored with me as Rory, and I shifted, turning my attention back to the skeptics.

"He was ready to forsake the crown to marry me," Rory said.

If I truly walked away from the crown, our lands would fall into anarchy. War would rain death on both our kingdoms. No, I was not willing to forsake my crown for her, as much as that pained my heart. But I was hellbent on having both the crown and Rory. There was no other way to bring peace to the region.

"I'm not willing to walk away from the crown or you," I said, making my intentions clear. "I have asked her to be my queen for more than just the practicality of a union between our kingdoms. She gives me hope and a sense of happiness that I have never felt in my entire life. If anything, she has enchanted me."

The one Rory called Felicity asked, "May I see your hand?"

I reached my hand out to her, and she took it and turned it over. She followed the lines on my palm with her finger, studying it as one would study a flower. Her brow creased, and she tilted her head, jerking her gaze up to mine. Her eyes widened, and she stepped back, exchanging an awed expression with the other two fae.

"Prince Zachary is Rory's fated mate," she gasped.

"It's actually King Zachary now," I corrected and stared at my palm, looking for exactly what Felicity had seen. Only skin with lines etched into it appeared. I dropped my hand and met her gaze. "Fated or not, I want Rory by my side, but I need to convince the elders to let go of the hate my mother poisoned them with."

The three fae exchanged glances and then said something in an unfamiliar language, sending a roll of sparkling magic toward the elders. I watched as it circled around the dragons and then all at once charged into them. Light filled their forms, and they gasped, arching their backs as black smoke bled from their skin, chased out by the light.

It was liberating to see my mother's poison squeezed out of the elders. They all blinked and looked down at their hands and arms, as if seeing themselves for the first time in ages.

"Do you think you could do that for the entire kingdom?" I asked them with a voice that held the awe I felt.

They blushed and shook their head. "We can only do that in small doses or in cases like this, where your mother's evil has such a tight grip that your wisdom can't penetrate."

The elders glanced around the room until their gaze fell on me and they all bent a knee, as if it had been me who released them from the darkness.

Little did they know, it was Rory who truly would release us all from the chains my mother put around us. I knew that with every fiber of my being.

"Azdok, will you please do me the honor of officiating my wedding?" I asked as they rose.

"Yes, Your Majesty," he said, without the nasty tone he had been using before.

Magic bloomed in the air, and I glanced at Rory. Her dress transformed into a beautiful wedding gown. One that was fit for a queen. I looked down to find my threads had changed as well. Rory was a vision in white, and I had my family's royal crest on my chest, along with the traditional marriage tunic of the Dragon Realm. I glanced at the fae with a nod and turned toward the vestibule to the side of the throne pedestal.

Azdok took his place in front of the altar. He picked up the sword from the mantel behind him and faced us.

"Swear you now, on this sacred blade, that there is no reason known to you that this union should not proceed." Azdok held out my father's sword, one hand on the ornate handle and the other holding the blade carefully.

Rory and I ran our index fingers along the edge of the blade, breaking the skin before we pressed our hands together, mingling our blood in a sacred union.

"I do so swear," we said in unison.

"Heavenly Father, creator of all things both in heaven and Earth, we humbly ask thee to bless this union. May these thy servants seek goodness all the days of their lives. May they be strong in defense of what is right, may they be united as one even as thou art with God. May they be numbered amongst thy sheep. We humbly pray in the name of the Father, and the Son, and the Holy Spirit. Amen."

Rory and I and the fae and other elders that gathered around us said, "Amen."

"Do you Zachary, King of the Dragon Realm take unto thyself, Aurora, Princess of the Kingdom of Light, as your lawful wife, and pledge unto her before God and these witnesses to be her protector, defender, and sure resort, to honor and sustain her, in sickness and in health, in fair and in foul, with all thy worldly powers, to cherish and forsaking all others, keep thee only unto her, so long as ye both shall live?"

Rory grinned up at me, and I nearly forgot there were other people in the room. When she lifted her eyebrow, I chuckled and nodded. "I will."

"Do you Aurora, Princess of the Kingdom of Light, take unto thyself King Zachary as your lawful husband and pledge unto him before God and these witnesses to honor and cherish him, to cleave unto him, in sickness and in health, in fair and in foul, be his one true and lasting counselor and solace, and forsaking all others, keep thee only unto him, so long as ye both shall live?"

"I will," Rory said, clear enough for the entire room to hear.

Azdok leaned close. "Do you have rings?"

I reached into my pocket, praying that the fae's magic had not made my parents' rings disappear. I had slid them into my pocket before we were shuttled to the coronation room for my induction to the throne. My fingers closed on them, and I smiled and nodded, handing them over to Azdok.

"Heavenly Father, bless these rings which King Zachary and Princess Aurora have set apart to be visible signs of the inward and spiritual bond which unites their hearts. As they give and receive these rings, may they testify to the world of the covenant made between them."

Azdok gave me my mother's ring, and I faced Rory.

"Rory, wear this ring as a symbol of my trust, my respect, and my love for you." I slid the ornate band on her finger, and to my surprise, it fit.

Azdok handed Rory my father's ring, and I held my left hand out for her.

"Zach, wear this ring as a symbol of my trust, my respect, and my love for you." Rory slid the ring on my finger.

"This circle will now seal the vows of this marriage and will symbolize the purity and endlessness of their love."

He glanced at both of us solemnly. "Thou hast pledged troth of thy own free will and sworn upon the Sword and exchanged rings as symbol of your binding love. May it be granted that what is done before God be not undone by man."

"Before I proclaim you joined, thou must kiss three times on cue."

I was ready for this part, and I pulled Rory against me, grinning down at her sparkling eyes.

"Once for luck."

I pecked her lips.

"Twice for love."

This time, my kiss lasted a little longer.

"Thrice for long life."

I'm not sure what I expected with the third kiss, but Rory held me tight, forcing me to twirl tongues and lose most of my mind in that single moment.

"By the power vested in me by the Dragon Realm, I now pronounce you husband and wife."

We were still kissing when Azdok announced us husband and wife, and the only reason I stopped was the whooping of the fae.

SPINDLE-A FRACTURED FAIRY TALE

SPINDLE Chapter 17

I PICKED RORY UP, walked out of the throne room, and headed to my chambers. Although I had made love to her back in her quarters in King Henrick's castle, I wanted to seal this marriage in my bed. I wanted to see Rory's face as she peaked and called out my name. I wanted her writhing under me.

But when I closed the door and put her on her feet, I never expected her to push me against the door. She kissed me with such fervor that I forgot to breathe. Before I knew it, my shirt was being ripped from my body.

Her mouth moved from mine, down my chin to my throat. Warmth followed like a trail of lava as she moved lower. My brain stalled as her hands undid my pants and yanked them down far enough to reveal my rock-hard member standing at attention.

Her sexy smile nearly undid me, but when her mouth covered the tip of my cock, I thought I had died and gone to heaven. This couldn't be real. My wife, on her knees in her beautiful wedding dress, looking like the hottest thing on earth.

I couldn't form words as she slowly stroked me with both her hands and her mouth. I threaded my hands in her hair and guided her as I leaned against the door for support, wondering what I did to deserve this.

Heat pooled in my belly, pulling from every cell. If she continued, I wouldn't be able to stop my eruption.

"Rory," I whispered gruffly.

She glanced up at me with worry lines creasing her forehead. "Am I not doing this right?"

I laughed in the face of such innocence. "You are doing it right. I just..."

She didn't let me finish speaking. She went back to sucking my cock. All it took was a few more strokes of her mouth before I lost it and held her head in place as I pushed my length into her mouth and exploded with a groan.

And the beauty at my feet swallowed every drop. When I pulled away, she gasped for breath and stared up at me with wide eyes and drops of my cum still glistening on her lips.

I leaned against the door and kicked off my pants. I scooped her up and carried her to my bed, pushing the fabric of her dress up almost until it reached her chin. Fabric swirled around her as I dove between her legs with only one thing on my mind: making Rory scream my name. And Lord help me, I nearly came again when she did. She writhed under me, and I kept going, bringing her to the brink again and again until her thighs were thick with her own juices. I tore the dress off her as violently as she had undressed me, but she pushed me onto my back and mounted me.

Rory rode me with abandon. Her body glistened with sweat, making the entire room enhanced with her sweet scent. Every muscle contracted with the strength of my next orgasm, and I nearly bucked her off. As soon as my tremors stopped, Rory fell over on top of me with a gasp. She laid with her head on my chest, her breath heaving just as strongly as mine.

I held her tightly to me and glanced over at the floor where our shredded clothing lay.

"I'm sorry about your wedding dress."

"It's just a dress," she said softly, her voice tickling my chest hairs. She rolled and snuggled into my side.

I closed my eyes and sighed. "We need to still face your father, assuming he takes my treaty offer seriously."

She lifted her head. "I really hope he does. It would be best for the citizens, who seem to be the ones first in line to die, like those farmers."

She was right. A peace treaty for both sides would give both kingdoms the type of prosperity that had been missing for twenty years. I could see the future, and it was going to be brighter than anyone ever expected.

A knock on the door interrupted my silent reverie. I covered Rory.

"Enter!" I called.

One of the castle guards pushed the door open and his eyes widened at the path of clothing before his gaze landed on us on the bed.

"Um, King Zachary, um. There seems to be a treaty delegation at the gates."

I smiled at Rory. "Let them in and get them some food. We will be down in a few minutes."

"Yes, Your Majesty."

After the door closed, I jumped out of the bed and rustled up some clothing for me. I glanced at Rory and then at her ruined clothing. "I'll send up the fae," I said. "In the meantime, you may clean up in my pool." I waved to the small tub in the adjoining room. "It's not as grand as the one in your father's castle..."

"It is perfect." She climbed out of bed and crossed to me, stood on her tiptoes, and caught a quick kiss before crossing to the bathtub.

I had to tear my gaze away from her perfect form. She was worthy of being called a goddess, and a worthy partner in ruling this kingdom, not to mention my lover for the rest of my life.

"It's time for peace," I whispered and set out to do just that. For Rory and for me.

The End

About J.E. Taylor

J.E. Taylor is a USA Today bestselling author, a publisher, an editor, a manuscript formatter, a mother, a wife, a business analyst, and a Supernatural fangirl. Not necessarily in that order. She first sat down to seriously write in February of 2007 after her daughter asked:

"Mom, if you could do anything, what would you do?"

From that moment on, she hasn't looked back.

Besides being co-owner of Novel Concept Publishing, Ms. Taylor also moonlights as a Senior Editor of Allegory, an online venue for Science Fiction, Fantasy and Horror. J.E. Taylor is also one of the co-hosts of the popular podcast Spilling Ink.

She lives in New Hampshire with her husband and two children and during the summer months enjoys her weekends on the shore in southern Maine.

Visit her at www.JEtaylor75.com and sign up for her newsletter for early previews of her upcoming books!

If you liked SPINDLE, you might also like these other fairy tales and magical romance stories from J.E. Taylor's backlist:

A FRACTURED FAIRY TALE

BOOKS 1-10

Little Red Riding Hood, Cinderella, Brave, Rapunzel, Frozen, Snow White, Sleeping Beauty, Aladdin, Beauty and the Beast and Peter Pan – all fairy tales you know and love, but twisted, fractured into something new.

Shifters and magic claw through the pages of these fractured fairy tales, giving you a thrilling take on an old tale.

Will the heroine survive whatever the evil villain has in store? Or will Love conquer all?

Grab your hardcover edition of A Fractured Fairy Tale—books 1-10 and find out!

A Fractured Fairy Tale books 1-10 includes

Red, Cinder, Brave, Tangled, Frozen, Snow, Spindle, Jasmine, Belle, Hook

Find these titles and other fantasy and suspense titles on J.E. Taylor's website!

https://JETaylor75.com

Milton Keynes UK
Ingram Content Group UK Ltd.
UKHW012247290324
440241UK00004B/178

9 798869 260642